TIDAL GRAVE

H.E. GOODHUE

For 'Sunset' Island

-1-

I'm going to crash the ferry. That's right. I'm going to drive in straight into the next boat I see...or better yet, maybe the jetty. Yes, the jetty. That's where the current is the strongest. No one will survive. Every asshole on this rusted hunk of crap will be pulled out to sea and sucked right out past the Atlantic Shelf. No one survives that. Yup, I'm definitely going to crash this ferry. Today is the day.

Raymond Weller promised himself this everyday as he started up the ferry. Ray, known to most as 'The Captain', hated his job and nickname with equal shares of rage. It wasn't the ferry's fault. Sure, she was little more than an open-air barge with a control tower in the center and space for about fifteen cars. And it was true that she was starting to look like there was more rust than white paint on her, but she was still a good boat. Ray just didn't want to captain the ferry that brought the self-important, city drones, escaping their high-rise hives for some R and R on Sunset Island, his island. Even worse than the doughy rich people were those worthless thirty-something year old children with their stupid clothes, thick glasses and beards. Ray had heard Jimmy call them hipsters, but he refused to call them that. There was nothing hip about being an unemployed bum. They were bearded and weirdoes, so 'beardoes' seemed like the appropriate term as far as Ray was concerned. But whatever you called them, they were the worst of the whole lot. No money other than their parents' credit cards. Gaggles of beardoes would pack into one of those annoying cars with a ZipCar sticker on the back because owning your own car was evidently not cool. They would arrive high on self-importance and God knew what else and then commence to act better than everyone else and treat everyone on the island like shit. These assholes would get drunk and cause problems that their parents would make disappear. Some shit teenage kid made the news by using bad parenting as a legal defense for killing people in a drunken boating accident three summers ago. The local papers had called it affluenza, like being an over-privileged, spoiled little shit was some kind of disease or something. Ray called it a steaming heap of horseshit. Bad parents, a lack of hugs or no rules or whatever that little turd used to get outta trouble, it was all crap. Ray figured what that kid needed was some time in a little prison cell and an ass whooping. But that didn't happen. What did happen was three families on Sunset Island had to bury children and the little monster that killed them got sent to a snooty rehab center, where he got to do yoga and ride fucking horses. Yes, sir, the beardoes were easily the worst part of the summer. At least the rich people had money and jobs. The only thing the beardoes had ever accomplished was spending a shit ton of daddy's money on looking homeless. Ray hoped a lot of them were on the ferry the day he finally decided to wreck it.

Some people on Sunset envied Ray's job. He got benefits from the town and didn't have to work when the water iced up. Ray thought they were idiots. Why would he want to be responsible for filling his island with the very thing he hated? Docking the ferry and unloading the tourists felt somewhat like dropping a flaming pile of dog turds on your own doorstep. Ray actually might have preferred the dog turds. Then again, dog turds didn't have deep pockets and fat wallets.

Sunset Island was little more than a rocky pile of sand held together by scrubby pines and inhabited by generations of salty folk who had called the island home for longer than anyone could remember. In its prime, Sunset had been a thriving fishing outpost. Being only ten miles from the Atlantic Shelf and deep water, along with all the large fish that swam there gave the inhabitants of Sunset a distinct advantage when it came to fishing. The shallow inlets surrounding the island had also been ideal for clamming and oysters. Families had thrived for generations on Sunset, embracing a simpler way of life. Then things changed.

Whether it was pollution or global warming or a pissed off King Neptune, Ray couldn't say. But what he did know was that the fish had disappeared and the clam beds had died. The fishing industry and Ray's way of life didn't follow too far behind.

Ray was born to be a fisherman, keyword being *was*. He went after big fish like marlin and tuna, the kind of fish you had to be a real man to land, the kind of fish you had to earn. Ray wasn't taught to do any of that pansy ass trawling where you just dragged a net along behind your boat and took whatever trash you pulled in. His father had told him that trawling was like walking into a bar, dropping your trousers and wiggling your worm about, waiting for the first sea cow willing to give it a nibble. You would land something, but it wouldn't be worth mounting.

No, Ray worked for his meals and money, just like his father and grandfather. Or at least he had until the fish vanished. Now, Ray found himself shuttling tourists from the mainland to Sunset Island. The trip was only about four miles roundtrip, but it felt like a lifetime of swallowing broken glass.

Some people hoped the new rig that went up a few months ago would breathe new life into Sunset Island. Ray knew better. They were out there drilling for something, not that they bothered to tell anyone on Sunset. The rig was doing something – something that required a lot of money. But none of that money was floating across the water to wash ashore on Sunset. No, the only thing they were going to get from the rig was problems, not that it stopped Mayor Billings from selling off the water rights to Glaxco Holdings.

Ray didn't really know any of the tourists enough to hate them, but driving around the island was all the knowledge he needed. Most people on Sunset Island lived in the middle of the island in small ranches and older homes – the kind of houses that said honest, hardworking people lived there. The outer ring of Sunset Island was dotted with newer construction. The kind of pre-fab crap castles that said money can buy a lot of things, but taste was certainly not one of them. Taking his boat around the island, Ray could see more and more of these pointlessly large houses blocking water views for everyone else.

There was no point in building a house that big. Why build something so big that you forgot whom you were living with?

Ray figured that maybe that was the point. But even if that was why these rich idiots built their monstrosities along the shoreline, it still seemed pointless. Most of the newer, larger houses on Sunset Island were empty nine to ten months out of the year. Rich people didn't like the cold, and they sure as hell couldn't hack the tough winters on Sunset. They would pop up like weeds for the warm months and disappear with the first gust of cold Atlantic air. Ray had learned to love the winters.

Whether or not Ray hated the tourists didn't matter. He needed them. Everyone on Sunset Island did. With fishing gone, tourism was one of the only industries left. Those two to three warm months, along with a little price gouging, brought in enough money to keep everyone on Sunset alive for another year.

The ferry bumped gently into the old rubber tires that lined the dock. Ray pulled the engines into reverse and swung the front gate of the ferry around. It rumbled into place and Ray put the engine in neutral. The front of the ferry dropped open, and cars, ones with names Ray couldn't pronounce, let alone afford, filed on.

A portly woman puffed her way up the narrow metal stairs leading to the control room. Her face was red and glistening like a baked ham. Layers of makeup did nothing to hide the ugliness in her eyes. Ray sighed and moved towards the door. There was a sign clearly asking passengers not to go past the red line painted at the bottom of the stairs, but this woman was either illiterate or didn't care. Ray figured it was more of the last, though he wouldn't rule out the first.

The woman's thick fingers, each spilling around garish gold rings like bread dough, rapped on the window.

"Captain!" the woman shrieked. "Captain! My children want a picture!"

Ray groaned as he slid out of the captain's chair. This was the part of his job he hated the most.

"I'll take the controls," Jimmy Horst grinned. Jimmy was Ray's second in command. He should have been a captain himself by this point, but Ray suspected that the photographic obligations kept Jimmy happily planted in the co-pilot's seat.

"Thanks, Jimmy," Ray sneered. He grabbed the handle and flung the door open. The woman impatiently tapped her foot on the metal landing. "Good afternoon, ma'am," Ray smiled with feigned cheer.

"Forgetting something?" the woman grunted as she thrust a thick finger towards Ray.

"Huh?" Ray mumbled.

"Here you go, *Captain!*" Jimmy laughed and tossed a white hat with gold braids like a Frisbee.

"Thanks again, Jimmy," Ray caught the hat.

"That's better," the woman nodded.

"Definitely an improvement, Captain," Jimmy laughed hysterically.

"Hey, Jimmy," Ray grumbled, "after we dock, why don't you go on down to the head and unclog it? Looks like some of the beardoes were eatin' Mexican last night." Now it was Ray's turn to laugh.

Maybe tomorrow I'll crash this tub, Ray thought as he made his was down the stairs to smile for another picture he would rather not take.

-2-

"Back it off!" Lou Sneltz screamed. Lou watched the pressure gauge shoot from yellow to red before the alarms started. Honestly, most of the time the stupid drill operated somewhere on the border between yellow and red, but full on red couldn't be ignored. The machinery, like the crew, was pushed to breaking, not that any of the suits from Glaxco Holdings cared. All they cared about was proving that this new drilling method worked and that it was possible to conduct underwater drilling at these depths.

Lou had been out on the rig for a month and still couldn't understand why they were testing the drill out where there was little to no chance of striking oil. Someone had muttered something about getting the water rights for dirt-cheap and not wanting to draw too much attention from the competition. Lou just wanted to finish his job, cash his check and get home to his wife and kid. The rest of the worrying was left for people way above his pay grade.

The pressure gauge dropped back down into the green. "Must have hit a pocket of gas or something," Lou called into his radio. "Let's see if we can't reach our mark by lunch." The deafening whir of machine let Lou know the control room agreed with his suggestion.

The rig vibrated as the massive drill bore deeper into the seabed. Lou had gotten used to the feeling of thousands of invisible bugs scurrying across him with tiny electric feet. Lou couldn't help but picture himself inside the power drill he kept in his garage.

A loud mechanical screech sounded from somewhere deep within the rig and the pressure gauge near flat lined into the red. Lou's hand shot out and slammed the kill button. The suits would be pissed about lost work time, but they'd be even more pissed if the drill broke.

"Had to kill it," Lou called. "Pressure gauge damn near broke. Back the bit off and let's give the seabed a few minutes to settle. Maybe the pressure knocked something loose."

Lou listened as the massive machine that controlled the drill groaned in frustration. The whole rig felt like it shuddered.

"Lou, this is control," the voice came through the intercom. *"Looks like the bit is stuck."*

"Stuck?" Lou asked. "Can you see on what or why? Try a few of the underwater cameras."

"Negative, Lou. The cameras are obscured. There appears to be seepage from the drill site and it's limiting visibility of the bit."

"Seepage?" Lou questioned. They were not anywhere near an oil deposit. How the hell could there be seepage? Lou quickly checked all his sensors. The drill appeared fine. No fluid leaks, all levels steady. It was just stuck. "Control, all fluid levels are steady. Any ideas what the seepage is from?"

"Negative, Lou. All we can see is black. Could be oil. We're notifying Glaxco headquarters. Stand by."

Lou switched on the screen that hung above his control panel. Inky black clouds swirled around the shaft of the drill. The bit vanished deep beneath the tendril that wound around it like smoke. Lou had been on more rigs and drill sites than he could remember, and struck oil on most of them, but it never had looked like this before.

"Lou, headquarters wants an ROV in the water immediately to assess the situation. We'll have one prepped and on deck for you."

"Control, this doesn't look like oil to me," Lou answered. "Have the images been relayed to headquarters? We might want to hold off on drilling until we figure out what's going on."

"Duly noted, Lou. Images were sent along with our original communication. Be advised that Glaxco headquarters has moved our status from experimental to operational. They want us pulling oil as soon as possible."

"Of course they do," Lou grunted as he pulled himself up the narrow ladder behind him.

-3-

Most businesses on Sunset Island were seasonal, closing down in the cold months. There was no point spending money on lights and heat for customers who weren't coming. Once the summer people abandoned Sunset, the town would close down, not much else open beyond the library and super market. The people of Sunset were tough and self-sufficient. The spas and designer cupcake stores were for ferry folk, not islanders.

The Dry Dock was one of the few businesses that maintained year round hours and patronage. It wasn't much more than a ramshackle shack at the intersection of two of the island's main roads. The blue clapboard sides had been covered with countless coats of blue paint, yet somehow still managed to never look clean. A small red rowboat with chipped paint and the name of the bar on the bow adorned the top of the building. Somehow, The Dry Dock managed to stay open year round. Maybe it was the owner Big Mo's dislike of tourists or maybe it was the fact that it was the only place to get drunk during the winter months, but whatever the reason, the locals loved The Dry Dock. Ray was no exception.

Every night after completing the ferry's final run back to the island and docking it, Ray would inevitably wander down to The Dry Dock to suck down a few beers while hiding from the tourist infestation.

Ray loved The Dry Dock and every salty bastard holed up in there. Hell, he felt more at home here than he did in his own house. The walls of The Dry Dock where covered with nautical memorabilia and framed newspaper clippings from the local paper. None of it was really important or impressive, but the low lights, watery beer and cluttered walls kept most of the ferry folk away. For that fact alone, Ray loved this place. Then of course, there was Big Mo. She wasn't the type of woman you wanted in your bed, but she was exactly the kind you wanted in your corner for a fight. Big Mo liked it that way. She once told Ray that someone had been crazy enough to ask her to marry him and she had hit him, hard. Big Mo was pretty sure he was dead and there was an outstanding warrant for her arrest.

Big Mo had a fiery tangle of red hair that brushed her wide shoulders and she must have stood a few inches over six feet. Her arms were as thick as bread loaves and covered with faded nautical tattoos. Ray had once told her that she looked custom made for The Dry Dock and Big Mo looked as if he had just told her she was the most beautiful woman in the world. Ray's drinks were on the house for a week after that.

"Hey, Ray," Big Mo nodded as he walked through the door. "Another fulfilling day captaining that plague ship of yours?"

"Swore today was gonna be the day," Ray grinned as he hoisted himself into his usual stool. "Yup, came this close to ramming her into the jetty today."

"Bet you did," Big Mo smiled and set a pint of beer in front of Ray. The beer looked strange and smelled even stranger.

"What the hell is this?" Ray examined the frosty glass. "Smells like one of those candles my wife used to have in the bathroom. All she ended up doing was makin' it smell like someone took a dump in a fruit basket."

"Classy as ever, Ray. Those guys over there said they wanted to buy the Captain a drink," Big Mo hooked her thumb towards a group of three beardoes at the other end of the bar. "I told 'em you wouldn't want any of that microbrew, fruit crap but they insisted."

"What the hell are they even doing here? Slumming or something?" Ray sniffed the beer. It reeked of artificial blueberries. "I ain't gonna drink this thing."

"You need to broaden your horizons, man," a guy clad in a flannel shirt, tight jeans and what looked like nurse's shoes said as he slid onto the stool next to Ray. "Expand your palate. Who knows, Captain, you might even like it. Imagine that, you going home buzzed and burping blueberries. How could your wife resist you then?"

"Not that it's any of your business, but my wife is gone, son," Ray pushed the beer away from him. "Mo, be a doll and bring me a Bud."

"I'm sorry, Captain," the beardo continued, "I didn't know your wife was gone. How'd it happen?"

"Ain't you a nosey one," Big Mo grunted as she put a new beer down in front of Ray. "Not like it's any of your business, but old Ray here lost his lady to the Big C, if you must know."

"Cancer?" the beardo asked. "Jeez, I'm sorry, Captain. I had a cat once that had something like that. It was super hard and like totally reshaped my view of the world."

"Wasn't cancer that took her, you moron," Ray took a slug from his beer and slammed the pint down on the bar.

"But she said… " the beardo protested.

"I said he lost his wife to the Big C," Big Mo cut it. "I didn't say nothing about cancer."

"Well then what's the Big C?" the beardo asked.

"More of a who than a what," Big Mo smirked. "Ray's wife Linda ain't dead kid, she's just a lesbian. Big C is the nickname Ray gave to his wife's new girlfriend, Carla. The two of them are shacked up together somewhere over on the mainland."

"Seemed easier to explain it that way," Ray shrugged and drained his pint glass. "Was your cat a lesbian too? Or can we stop pretending that we have anything to talk about?"

"Look, man, my apologies about the wife and beer. Let me buy your next round, Captain," the beardo offered.

"Son, I'm gonna let you buy me that beer because I figure it's the least you could do for wasting my time, but if you don't stop calling me Captain and I'm gonna smash the pint glass upside your hairy head," Ray stated flatly.

"You got it, Cap – I mean Ray," the beardo nodded. "Two more Buds please."

Big Mo set the next round down and then shuffled off to tend to the rest of the beardoes who had thankfully stayed at the other end of the bar.

"So what do you want? A picture or something? Cuz I left that stupid fuckin' hat on the ferry," Ray asked before letting out a thunderous belch.

"No, no," the beardo shook his shaggy head. "My name is Alex and those are my friends down there. We were hoping to hire you for a job."

"Hire me?" Ray snapped. "What the hell are you talking about, kid? I drive the ferry from point A to point B and then back to A again. It ain't some damn pleasure cruise."

"We didn't want to use the ferry," Alex explained. "We wanted to go sightseeing over by Peach Island and maybe the new rig. Thought maybe we could charter a boat with you."

Ray sighed. Every so often, some of the beardoes would ask about chartering a boat over to Peach Island. It wasn't much to see, just an empty stretch of sand and some trees. But the remains of an abandoned US Military Infectious Disease Laboratory tempted all of the assholes looking to take black and white photos of some shit no one cared about. Ray never could figure out why black and white made a photo of trash into art, instead of just a two-tone picture of junk. But the rig was a new request.

"Kid, all that crap you read on the internet about monsters and mutants on Peach Island is just that – crap. The government wasn't studying anything more than some stuff that made a whole bunch of livestock sick. There's nothing to see," Ray slid his glass over so Big Mo could refill it. "There ain't nothing there but some old buildings and overgrown trees. You wanna take pictures of shit like that, I'll gladly point you towards my neighbor's house."

"What about the rig?" Alex persisted.

"What about it?" Ray shrugged. "Ain't shit to see there either. Besides, puttering around near that thing ain't going to make them Glaxco boys too happy. They got guns on that thing, kid, and won't think twice bout firing one across the bow. You best just stay right here on Sunset where you can't get into no trouble. I thank you for the beers, but I won't be driving you over near that rig."

"Fine," Alex snapped. He was obviously unaccustomed to not getting his way. Ray wondered if he was going to have to watch a thirty-year-old man have a temper tantrum. "Well, then we'll just rent a boat and drive ourselves."

"Wouldn't recommend that either, kid," Ray took a sip from his new beer. "That rig is out past where the shelf drops off. Water gets mighty deep and waves can come outta nowhere. Nope, you don't want to be out there with no boating experience under your belt."

"Boating experience?" Alex scoffed. "I spent my summers sailing. We'll be just fine."

"All due respect there, Alex," Ray snorted, "but you farting around in a six foot Sunfish on a glassy pond don't really count as boating experience. Might count towards a badge or something like that at summer camp, but it don't mean much out past where the shelf drops off."

"Like I said," Alex pushed away the bar, "we'll be just fine."

"Suit yourself, kid," Ray turned back to his beer. "It's your funeral."

Ray had no idea how right he was.

-4-

Lou stood on the edge of the rig and watched the ROV disappear beneath the water. He knew it was a machine, but oddly, still found himself worrying about it. Maybe he had been out on the rig too long? Maybe he just missed his kid and was putting his stored up emotions into a little remote controlled submarine.

"Alright, let's see what the hell is going on down there," Lou grumbled as he sat down behind the control panel. He tested the controls, found everything to be in working order and fired up the engines.

A swirling mass of bubbles danced across Lou's screen, but soon disappeared. This was normal when the engines first kicked on. The ROV dove deeper into the black water, following the shaft of the drill. Lou would stop the ROV and periodically check the drill. It looked fine. There were no signs of damage, no indication that it had sprung a leak.

Thick tendrils of black twisted away from where the drill bore into the seabed. Lou pulled back on the ROV's throttle and let the little submarine float for a few seconds. Something was strange, seemed off. Then it dawned on Lou.

"Where the hell are the fish?" Lou wondered aloud. Granted, he didn't expect to see shimmering schools of fish this deep, but a jellyfish or angler wouldn't have been out of the question. But Lou's screen was devoid of life, not a single plant, sponge or tubeworm was to be found.

The ROV dropped closer to the drill site. Everything looked normal. There didn't appear to be any obvious reason why the drill would be stuck.

"Control, try firing up the drill and backing it out slowly," Lou called into his radio. He heard the machinery fire up and watched the drill buck, but it didn't move.

"Lou, this is Control. The drill is still stuck. Please advise."

"Bring it up to full and try pushing forward. Maybe we'll be able to knock it loose," Lou said.

The whole rig felt like it was vibrating as the drill came on at full. Lou watched his screen as the pipe guiding the drill bucked and bounced about. The black liquid began weeping from the drill site with more intensity.

"Control, shut it down," Lou called. "Let me move the ROV in to check the site. It looks like more oil is seeping out. We don't want a Gulf incident on our hands, so let's be careful here."

"Understood."

Lou guided the ROV to the sea floor. The drill site looked normal. Once he was in position, Lou grabbed the control for the ROV's mechanical arm. It wasn't strong, but would be enough to move a few rocks around and maybe give Lou a peek at whatever was causing the problem.

Shifting aside a few piles of rocks and sand provided Lou with no new ideas. He guided the ROV around to the other side and continued to investigate. Still nothing.

A large cloud of the black liquid clouded Lou's screen.

"Shit! Control, it looks like we have the beginnings of a major leak on our hands. Advise the crew and headquarters that we are going to need to cap this site. I recommend we do it quick too, because it looks like more oil is seeping out. We need to get this under control before the EPA notices."

"Got it, Lou. Just let us send word to headquarters and get the go ahead. Please stand by."

The screen filled with more of the inky liquid spilling out from the sides of the drill. Lou had handled his share of oil leaks and this looked manageable, but things could change in the blink of an eye.

Bubbles began erupting from the drill site, further obscuring Lou's view of the situation.

"Control, you better get the okay sooner rather than later," Lou warned. "Looks like we ruptured a gas pocket or something. We've got a lot of activity at the drill site."

"Understood, Lou. We're working on it. Please stand by."

Working on it? What the hell was there to work on? If they didn't get a concrete cap down there ASAP there was going to be an environmental disaster and PR nightmare on Glaxco's hands.

Lou switched on the extra floodlights on the sides of the ROV. His screen was suddenly washed out with red.

"Control, it looks like we're having some sort of technical problems with the ROV's cameras. The screen went red when I switched on the floodlights." Lou tried pushing a few buttons, but the screen remained a steady sheet of dark red.

Bubbles perforated the blanket of red that clouded Lou's screen.

"Uh, Control, I'm not sure what we hit down there, but I don't think it's oil," Lou called into his radio.

If there was a response from Control, Lou would never know because moments after his transmission, the entire rig began to violently tremble and shake. Barrels, machinery and people tumbled across the deck of the rig as it pitched to the left. Seconds later, it righted itself, leaving no trace of what had only just happened aside from the mess and injured people strewn across its deck.

Somehow, Lou had remained at the controls of the ROV. People yelled for help, but he felt compelled to watch the feed from the little submarine. The red appeared to have thinned out, giving Lou enough visibility to make out the drill site.

The rocks around the guide pipe shifted as something pushed upwards. The ROV struggled to remain in place as a series of massive bubbles shook the small vehicle. Lou spun the camera to try and see what was causing the disturbance. A large section of the guide pipe buckled and collapsed, almost crushing the ROV.

"Holy shit," Lou gasped. The ground beneath the drill site suddenly caved in, leaving a huge crater in the sea floor. The crater bowed outward and pulsed. Bubbles erupted between the rocks and carried clouds of sand and dirt into the water.

A massive chasm yawned where the drill site once had been.

"Control, we have a full on collapse occurring at the drill site," Lou called. "Visibility is almost at zero due to debris, but we lost the drill. Good news is I don't see any more oil seeping out."

"Lou, Glaxco headquarters wants you to investigate with the ROV. Figure out what the hell happened to the drill."

Lou guided the ROV closer to the giant hole in the seabed. It looked like the drill had punctured an underwater cave. Lou knew the ocean was littered with caves like this, but he had never seen one this massive.

"Control, we appear to have broken through into a massive underwater cave," Lou reported. "The ROV is right on the edge and I still can't see anything. I'd recommend that we – holy shit!" The cave suddenly widened, enveloping the entire view of the ROV's camera in black. Now all Lou could see was static.

"Report, Lou. Could be wrong, but I don't think holy shit is going to cut it with headquarters. They need answers."

"Control, there must have been a cave in or something. I'm not really sure, but we just lost the feed from the ROV. I think it's gone completely. Wait! I can see something, but ROV is unresponsive. Stand by, control."

Lou watched as a grainy image appeared on his screen. It was dark inside the cave and what little he could see was pinkish red and pulsating. Why the hell would a cave pulsate?

"Control, I'm not sure what I'm looking at right now. The image is completely degraded, but it looks like the inside of the cave is…well, it looks like it might be alive."

"Alive? Lou, what the hell are you talking about?"

"I wish I knew," Lou answered honestly.

The rig shifted again, this time tilting to the right. Metal screeched in protest as the supports that held the rig in place bent and snapped. Lou ducked as things sailed past his head. He grabbed the side of the ROV control panel and tried to remain safe, but never saw the toolbox heading directly for him.

A dull metallic *thunk* was all Lou heard before pain exploded throughout his head. He could feel something warm running down the side of his head. He could feel himself sliding towards the edge of the rig, but seemed unable to stop himself.

Lou rolled onto his back and watched with a dumbfounded fascination as the cave he had seen through the ROV camera yawned beneath him in the water. *How could a cave move?* Lou wondered. *What happened to ROV?*

Lou wouldn't have to wait long for an answer. He would find out firsthand exactly what happened to the ROV.

-5-

"Stupid townie ferry boat captain," Alex seethed as he fired up the engine on the Bayliner he had rented. Sure, he told the guy at the boat rental that he and his friends were going fishing, but why bother confusing these yokels with the truth? The guy got his money and Alex got his boat so that was all that mattered.

Alex's three friends languished in the back of the boat. A night of hardcore drinking followed by a morning spent in the sun on the open water didn't appear to be mixing well. Wally, Alex's roommate, lay over the side violently spewing blueberry scented vomit into the wind.

"Wally! Don't get that shit on the boat, man," Alex yelled. "My dad is going to be super pissed if he sees a charge for cleaning the boat on top of the rental fee. Be cool, man."

"Your dad doesn't even read the damn statement," Wally protested before another gush of upchuck sailed into the breeze.

"Whatever, dude," Alex waved his hand dismissively at his three friends. Jo-Jo and Auggie were passed out and Wally was busy puking, but Alex was determined to enjoy his day.

Granted, the townie ferryboat captain had been right about Peach Island. Alex wanted mutated government mishaps. What he found were other hipsters and a few crumbling buildings covered in vines. Alex wanted to explore something new, something other hipsters would marvel at and that certainly wasn't Peach Island. But the rig was a completely different story.

Alex hadn't told anyone, other than the Captain, about his plans to visit the rig, not even his friends. So Alex had loaded up his hung over compatriots, waved goodbye to Peach Island and headed out towards the open water and the rig.

"Where the frig are we going?" Wally groaned from the back of the boat.

"Just shut up and have a beer or something," Alex shouted over the wind. What he would never tell his friends is that he was secretly beginning to think this adventure might have been a bad idea. The waves were much larger out here and appeared out of nowhere. But fuck the waves. Alex was going to navigate to the rig, take some pictures, then go back to The Dry Dock, and shove them right up the Captain's wrinkled ass.

Something bounced off the hull of the Bayliner as Alex pushed it over the top a wave. A second *clunk* and then a third followed close behind. Alex pulled the throttle back. The boat lurched forward as the wake it trailed caught up with the back end. As the engine softly chugged, the boat idled in the middle of the open water.

Alex scanned the horizon. Where the hell was the rig? He remembered someone at summer camp saying that it was hard to judge distances on the water, but he was sure he should be close to the damn rig.

Another hollow *thunk* echoed off the hull of the boat.

"Man, what the hell is that noise?" Wally moaned. He held the sides of his head and then puked over the side. Wally coughed a few times and looked up, while still hanging over the edge of the boat. "Dude, whatever that noise is, it's killing me."

Alex turned to yell at Wally, and tell him to stop being such a whiny bitch. Alex needed to vent his anger on someone and it sure as all hell was not going to be directed at himself. "Wally, why don't you go and check your backpack for a maxi pad or something." But there was no answer, only a loud splash.

Running to the back of the boat, Alex had to leap over his two sleeping friends. How could Wally be so stupid? Had he really just fallen into the ocean?

"Good, that'll teach you to stop being such a princess," Alex grinned as he reached over the side of the boat expecting to see Wally stupidly treading water beside it. Wally was not there.

Shit! Shit! Shit! Alex screamed inside his head. If Wally hit his head, he could be knocked out and sinking right now. Forget explaining the cost of a boat cleaning, how the hell was

Alex going to explain the cost of a good defense attorney to his father? This was bad, like jail bad.

"Wally, you dumb shit, stop fucking around!" Alex yelled. He expected, no hoped, that Wally would surface any minute now with that stupid grin stretched across his face, but there was nothing, only the gentle sound of the waves lapping against the side of the boat and the hollow *clunk* of something hitting its hull.

"What the fuck is that noise?" Alex almost screamed as he heard something hit the bottom of the Bayliner yet again. Reaching over the side of the boat, Alex grabbed what looked like the offending object. "What is this? Driftwood or something?" He pulled the debris onto the boat. It was a splintered length of wood with the letters 'GLAX' painted across it. The end had been broken. No, not broken. It was chewed.

"Glaxco?" Alex wondered aloud. Wasn't that the name of the company the Captain had mentioned? Was this garbage from the rig? No, it couldn't be. There was no way an oil company was going to pollute with garbage that had their name written right across it – that would just be stupid. But then if it wasn't garbage from the rig, could it be part of it?

This was where the rig was supposed to be, Alex was sure of that. But then where the hell was it? Furthermore, where the hell was Wally?

"Oh shit! Wally!" Alex rushed back to the side of the boat. Something bobbed in the trough of a few rolling waves. A pair of stained white Keds waved to Alex as they rode down the next wave. "Damn it, Wally, you dumb shit. I'm not going to jail for you." Alex kicked off his shoes and leapt from the side of the Bayliner. He was captain of the swim team when he was in high school, so surely he could swim over to Wally's stupid ass and drag him back to the boat. Hell, Alex would be a hero. That was a story. Try and top that.

Alex pushed through the waves. More debris floated around him. Some of it had the logo for Glaxco Holdings printed on the sides. The rest of it just looked like junk, but Alex couldn't shake the feeling that something major had gone down on the rig. A smile broke across his face. Now, not only would he be a hero for saving his friend, but also would be the first person to break the news about a major accident at Glaxco Holding's new rig. The traffic on his blog would explode, and forget about his Twitter and Instagram followers – they would triple easily after he started posting pictures of this. All he had to do first was drag Wally's dumb ass back to the boat.

Alex looked over his shoulder to make sure the boat wasn't drifting away. It looked fine. Jo-Jo and Auggie were still passed out in the back. Bubbles began breaking the surface around the hull of the boat. At first, it was only a handful, nothing really, but soon it looked like the sea was boiling beneath the boat.

Shit! The boat must have a leak or something! Alex thought. What the hell were they going to do now? Wally was only a few feet away, but the dumb ass looked like he was headfirst under water. Only Wally could drown while floating.

Kicking harder and riding a swell, Alex grabbed Wally's ankle and pulled. He turned to swim back to the boat and saw that the water around it was now a frothing stew of debris and bubbles.

A massive shadow passed under the boat and Alex felt fear squeeze his heart. Was it a shark? No, no way there was a shark that big. Maybe it was a whale or something? Didn't they use bubbles to catch fish? Alex thought he remembered something on Animal Planet about that, but then again, he only watched Animal Planet when he was stoned.

The shadow darkened the water beneath the boat. The water swelled and lifted the boat upwards. Something dark and huge broke through the water from both sides. Water streamed off the sides, obscuring any details beyond size. Fiberglass splintered and broke as the boat was pulled beneath the water. The engines chugged a few more times before disappearing beneath the waves. The boat was gone. Auggie and Jo-Jo were gone.

Alex wanted to panic. He wanted to cry. He should have listened to that crusty old townie that drove the ferry. What kind of whale would eat a fucking boat? You'd think that was the kind of thing that rat bastard the Captain would have thought to have warned him about.

"Damn it, Wally! Wake the fuck up! Wake up!" Alex screamed as he shook his friend's ankle. Alex pulled Wally towards him, suddenly realizing that Wally's considerable beer gut should have made it more difficult than it was.

The top half of Wally was gone. Ragged strips of skin danced in the water. A long, ropey coil of intestine spilled out and trailed downward, disappearing in the murky depths of the sea.

Seeing the remains of his friend, Alex began to cry and wet his pants. He figured that it really didn't matter since he was in the water, so he didn't really try to fight it.

This was the Captain's fault. All of it fell on his shoulders. Why the hell wouldn't he have warned Alex that there was something out here that could do this to a person or a boat? Maybe he didn't know. Maybe it no longer mattered.

Alex watched as the shadow he had seen beneath the boat took shape beneath him. It filled his field of vision and swelled to unimaginable proportions. As the shadow twisted upwards, Alex let out a weak cry and vanished beneath the waves.

Carson Creswell IV was perhaps the only member of the Creswell family that looked forward to summering on Sunset Island. His older sister and brother were always too tired from the night before to have any real fun. The kind of fun they had made them smell funny and act grumpy, even though they slept most of the day. And then there was Mom and Dad. They were too busy trying to avoid each other to notice anything that Carson was doing.

But things had been like this for every summer Carson could remember, and eventually, he learned to love the freedom. He could slip out the back door of his family's massive, beachfront summer home and be free to explore. The beach always held wonders and excitement for a young Carson. There had been that one year when he found a dried out horseshoe crab. It smelled awful, but looked so cool and prehistoric. His sister had never screamed so loud in her whole life after Carson snuck the horseshoe crab into her bed. Sure, his sister was mad, but what she going to do, tell their mom? Everyone knew she was at yacht club and probably wasn't going home anytime soon, at least not her home.

Carson meandered down the beach. It was early and still quiet. Soon, other people would begin to wander out of their houses, some kids, but never really anyone who Carson wanted to play with. The other kids were boring. They never wanted to explore or find things.

A large shadowy lump flopped on the beach a few hundred feet from Carson. At first, he thought he might have stumbled across their neighbor, Mr. Van Bolden, wrestling with the waitress from the yacht club again. The waitress was losing from what Carson could tell, but she didn't look like she was really trying. Mr. Van Bolden was old and fat and Carson figured he should've been pretty easy to beat. Carson also thought it seemed silly to wrestle somebody naked, but his dad said that was something adults did once in a while for fun or love. Carson figured his dad and mom might have been in better moods if they tried wrestling once in awhile – it sure seemed to make Mr. Van Bolden happy, but the waitress not so much.

Getting closer, Carson could see that the shadow was thankfully not a naked Mr. Van Bolden. It wasn't even a person at all. No, Carson had stumbled upon perhaps the most amazing thing he had ever found washed up on Sunset Beach.

A large gray shark thrashed a few times in the sand, as if trying to pull itself further onto land. Carson knew better than to get close to it, but couldn't pull himself away. The shark was bigger than any he had ever seen, easily five feet long. Carson thought it might be a sandbar shark but couldn't be sure without his books. But really, the type of shark didn't matter because *it was a shark!* That alone was awesome!

Watching the shark was incredible, but as Carson's gaze settled on the shark's gills, he felt his heart tighten. His books had taught him about this. Sometimes animals like sharks or dolphins or whales would get sick and beach themselves. Most of the time, there was nothing anyone could do. Carson could see this shark was going to die.

Perhaps it was youth, stupidity, or maybe a combination of the two, but Carson couldn't watch this amazing animal die. The shark's black glassy eyes followed Carson as he walked carefully around behind it. The shark was too weak to fight as Carson grabbed its tail and began pulling it back to the water. The shark's skin was rough and dry, and it scraped Carson's soft hands, but he held tight. He was going to save the shark and watch it swim a way. No would ever believe him, but that wouldn't matter. He'd know the truth.

Carson had pulled the shark out into shin deep water when it began to thrash and knocked him backwards into the ocean.

"What are you doing, you big dummy?" Carson shouted as he rubbed the salt water from his eyes. "I was trying to save you!"

The shark had already driven itself back onto the beach.

Something told Carson to turn around, and look out across the water. He froze.

A series of large black fins, some triangular and others curved back, all headed for the beach. Carson watched in amazement as dolphins and sharks glided through the water, past his legs and onto the beach. Their bodies covered the beach.

Carson rushed back to his house. Hopefully, someone would be up that might know what was going on. Maybe his dad would know why the sharks and dolphins were on the beach. It seemed like something a dad should know.

Why were they all killing themselves? Carson had tried to help the shark, but it just broke free and swam back onto the beach. His books must be wrong. Carson knew they were. That shark wasn't sick. No, it was scared.

-7-

One of the few benefits of being the ferry captain was that Ray had a bank of sick days and a second in command to run the boat. Honestly, Ray couldn't remember the last time he was actually sick. Hung over was damn pretty close though, so he wasn't feeling overly conflicted about calling out of work. Sure, Sunset Island was so small that Ray would run into his boss at some point, but screw him. He was out more than Ray ever was and was twice as drunk when he finally did show up. Nope, Ray had earned a day off as far as he was concerned.

Sitting around and watching daytime television was never really Ray's thing. He had tried to get into those talk shows and crapfests about 'real' housewives when his wife was around, but it only ever pissed him off. Ultimately, Ray would get bored and make a comment about one of the big boobed, plastic monsters and Linda would get mad. Fighting would follow close behind. Ray kind of thought it was funny that reality TV shows would be the downfall of his marriage, but there you had it. Wherever Linda was, Ray hoped that the Big C liked watching those stupid shows, because lord knew he wasn't going to and God bless the woman if she would.

Sunset Island didn't take very long to travel around and after his third lap in his beat up old pick up, Ray was bored enough to wander into the hardware store. Like most businesses on Sunset, the hardware store was a kind of jack-of-all-trades. They sold actual tools and lumber, but also had a large variety of adult videos, beach toys and a boat rental under the same roof. Ray didn't know what he wanted, but figured he could probably find it at that hardware store. Besides, the owner Cal was always good for a conversation about the latest island news.

"Hey ya, Ray," Cal waved as the tinny jingle of bells announced Ray's arrival.

"What's the good word, Cal?" Ray asked. This was how they started every conversation.

"Good word? Shit, I don't know about that," Cal scoffed, "but Lord knows I got plenty of bad ones for that little shit that rented my Bayliner and hasn't brought it back yet."

"Your Bayliner is missing?" Ray asked.

"Almost half a day overdue," Cal nodded. "One of them…what'd you call them? Beardoes! Yeah, that's your word! One of them beardoes rented it with a couple of his friends to do some fishing. Shit, I should'a known better by the looks of them. Those little turds were more likely to catch the clap than a damn fish. But shit, Ray, you know how it is. Them ferry folk got money and we need it."

"Ain't that the truth," Ray agreed. "You wouldn't happen to know if the beardo that rented your boat was named Alex, would you?"

"Sure," Cal pulled a stack of yellow carbon copy papers from under the counter and slipped off the rubber band holding them together. He flipped through a few and then pulled one free. "Yes sir! That little turd was most certainly named Alex. How'd you know, Ray?"

"Figured it was him," Ray answered. "A while back he was hanging around The Dry Dock trying to get me to take him and his friends out to Peach Island and the Glaxco rig. I told him to piss off, but he seemed pretty determined."

"Well, shit on me," Cal exhaled. "Peach Island ain't nothing new, but Lord knows what that asshole coulda done to my boat out in the deep water round the rig."

"Hey, you want me to do a lap round the island and check for signs of your boat? I could swing by Peach Island too. I bet that idiot is there drunk and passed out on the beach with the rest of those morons." Ray offered.

"That'd be much appreciated," Cal said. "But you sure you want to do that?"

"I was bored and looking for something to keep me occupied today anyways, so why the hell not?" Ray shrugged.

"Cuz there's one bitch of a storm rolling our way," Cal pointed towards the muted weather report playing on the TV hung above the counter. "Ain't you heard that the weather is making all the fish crazy, driving them nuts. I hear tell that a whole shit ton of sharks and dolphins beached themselves this morning over at Sunset Beach. Must'a been one hell of a sight to see all them rich folk waking up to see their expensive private beach covered with a whole shit ton of dead fish."

"Sure it was," Ray nodded.

"But regardless of the dead fish fucking up some rich peoples' day," Cal continued, "that's gotta be one hell of a storm to drive all them critters on to land."

"I'll be quick about it," Ray laughed. "Hell, what's the worst that could happen?"

-8-

URGENT- MARINE WEATHER MESSAGE...A hurricane warning has been issued. The National Hurricane Center and National Weather Service reports a major storm front moving towards the Eastern US seaboard. Expect hurricane strength winds in excess of 93 Knots, storm surges and heavy rainfall. Coastal waters are expected to rise significantly. Commercial vessels should prepare for very strong winds and dangerous sea conditions. All ships are advised to remain in port or seek shelter in the nearest port until winds and waves subside.

"Captain Bertrand sir, did you hear that?" First mate François Dubois asked. The message repeated through the radio and flashed across the screen in text form. The cargo ship *Ponce De Leon* had traveled from the Caribbean up the Eastern seaboard with a series of stops, but now found itself in between ports.

"I most certainly did, Mr. Dubois," Captain Bertrand nodded. "We have two options. Stay the course and hope that we can ride it out in open water or seek the nearest port."

"With all due respect, Captain, sir, I'm not sure this is the type of storm we want to face in open water. We've unloaded most of our cargo, so the ship is riding higher in the water than usual, sir. The wind alone would be trouble, but no doubt a rogue wave could flip the ship, sir." Dubois checked the warning message again. "There are a few small islands within our proximity, sir. The closest island is one called Sunset Island, Captain. The surrounding waters are deep enough to accommodate the ship, sir."

"Agreed, Mr. Dubois," Captain Bertrand turned to the radio operator. "Notify the Ministry of Transport that we will be dropping anchor near Sunset Island. It is small, but very close to deep water and we should be safe riding out the storm there."

-9-

Forget gimmicky pills or sports drinks. The only real cure for a hangover was black coffee and sea air as far as Ray was concerned, but right now, the ocean seemed to have a differing of opinions.

Small waves battered the sides of Ray's twenty-one foot open body aluminum boat. It had an oversized seventy-five horsepower Mercury engine on the back and was painted a drab olive green. The interior of the boat was little more than three wooden benches, a large red gas tank and an endless series of mud stains. In his younger years, Ray had used the boat to go clamming, but since the beds had died, the boat had spent most of its time moored at the end of Ray's street. It had been years since a single clam had clattered to the bottom of the boat, yet it still somehow clung to the undeniable fart-like stench that rose from the flats. Oddly enough, the methane funk reminded Ray of better, happier times.

The boat launched itself off the crest of a large wave, causing the engine to growl with abandon, as the prop broke free of the water. Ray lost control of the boat for a moment and swung out in a wide fishtail that sent a froth arc of seawater sloshing sideways. He couldn't help but smile.

Ray cut the engine back as he approached Peach Island. A few rental boats dotted the beach, no doubt having been run aground by those idiot beardoes. Ray checked each boat, but none was Cal's missing Bayliner.

Ray turned towards the shore and gunned the engine. He cut it when he came within a few feet of shore and glided onto the beach. A few beardoes stumbled towards Ray's boat. At moments like these Ray really wished the urban legends about Peach Island were true. Seeing the approaching beardo mauled by some government created monster would have been priceless. Alas, no monsters were on the island, aside from those created by absentee parents and oversized trust funds.

"Hey man," a beardo in an old timey red and white striped bathing suit waved. The swimsuit reminded Ray of the old sepia pictures that hung in the halls of the Sunset Library. The pictures were from the early 1900s. This idiot was not. These morons were certainly desperate to do anything to get noticed.

"Hey yourself," Ray grunted as he hopped down from the bow of his boat. "Is Alex around?" Ray momentarily thought about giving a description of Alex, but realized that the details would fit just about every asshole on Peach Island. "He was driving a Bayliner. You know, big fishing boat with a double engine on the back. I think he had three other guys with him."

Swimsuit thought for a second and scratched his bread. "Yeah! Oh yeah!"

"So he's here?" Ray wondered if he had just missed the boat on his way around Peach Island.

"Um, nope," Swimsuit shook his head like a dog emerging from the water.

Ray swallowed his anger and desire to bury this kid headfirst in the sand. "Look, kid, I'm gonna say this real slow so you can follow it." Swimsuit nodded again. "Is Alex here, like on the island right now?"

"Um, nope," Swimsuit said again.

"Jeez, kid, your mom and dad must be real proud of you." Ray balled his hands into fists. "Would ya mind tellin' me where the hell he is?"

"Sure man," Swimsuit grinned. "He left."

Ray let out a sound of pure frustration and weakening self-control. "And where did he go?" Ray spat through gnashed teeth.

"That way," Swimsuit pointed out towards the open water. Ray had hoped that Alex and his friends wouldn't be stupid enough to go out to the Glaxco rig, and that maybe they would get distracted on Peach Island. He saw now that his hope was misplaced.

"Okay, thanks, kid," Ray started walking back towards his boat and stopped, and turned back to Swimsuit. "Hey, kid, there's one bitch of a storm on its way. You and your hairy friends should haul ass back to wherever it is you came from. This ain't gon' be any weather to be sleeping out under the stars."

"No worries, dude," Swimsuit waved. "I was like a Boy Scout for like six months and I totally have a sweet ass tent. I'm set."

"I'd pack that *sweet ass tent* up quick and get the hell on home, but I guess it's your funeral, kid," Ray yelled over the roar of his engine.

Ray noticed he had been using that phrase a lot as of late. He turned towards the Glaxco rig and gunned the engine.

-10-

The *Ponce De Leon* drifted a few miles away from Sunset Island and Peach Island. Dubois had insisted that they move the ship closer to land, but the last thing Captain Bertrand wanted was to deal with nosey locals or worse yet, risk having the storm waves run the ship aground.

"Mr. Dubois, please do a quick inspection of the deck and ensure that everything is stable and tied down." Captain Bertrand watched the wall of gray moving across the water. The entire horizon and sky were eaten by the metallic mass of clouds. The storm was going to be huge.

"Yes, Captain," Dubois nodded and slipped out onto the narrow walkway surrounding the super structure. Dubois could already feel the wind beginning to whip and pull at his uniform. He hoped they would be safe.

Starting in the stern and working forward, Dubois checked and rechecked anything that could come loose and become a projectile in the storm. Everything looked good.

As he knelt to check a few knots, the wind gusted and ripped Dubois hat from his head. He leapt and stretched over the side, grasping the brim between his thumb and pointer finger. Dubois let out a breath he hadn't realized he was holding. He pulled his hat firmly back onto his head and waggled his finger at the water below. "Not today, my mischievous friend. No, you will need to rely on natural beauty and not fashion." Dubois chuckled at his own corny joke. He loved being at sea. He loved the ocean, even on days like these where he knew it wasn't going to love him in return.

A series of waves moved towards the *Ponce De Leon*. They were large, an eight-foot face or bigger on each, but nothing that would cause a ship of this size any trouble. Dubois watched the waves with an odd fascination. Something was wrong, but he couldn't exactly say what.

It slowly dawned on Dubois that the waves were moving opposite to all others. Not only that, but they were significantly larger than any of the surrounding white caps.

"What the hell?" Dubois muttered, as the waves appeared to pick up speed and surge higher. Something dark was moving beneath them. He grabbed the radio that hung from his shoulder and called the deck. "Captain I believe we have something heading towards the ship, sir. Maybe a submarine. Is there anything on the sonar?"

"Dubois, you have to be mistaken," Captain Bertrand answered. "There is no way a submarine would ping this large on the sonar. Are you sure it's not a pod of whales?"

Leaning over the deck, Dubois saw something large and yellow glowing just beneath the waves. It disappeared and then reappeared closer to the ship. He had no idea what he was looking at, but he could have sworn it resembled a massive eye.

The waves disappeared against the hull of the ship. Dubois shook his head, convinced he was hallucinating. A loud splash drew his attention to the water once again.

A muscular greenish black pillar rose from beneath the water and towered over the ship. Water cascaded downward like a shower of glass before rippling across the frothing sea. It tapered to a sharp point and was ridged with a set of wicked looking spikes. This thing was easily the length of the ship and most definitely, something Dubois had never witnessed before. The tip flicked back and forth, as if attempting to bat the clouds playfully.

A spray of cold ocean water shook Dubois from his state of shock and awe. He turned to sprint back to the super structure.

"Captain!" Dubois wheezed into the radio. "Captain, it's not whales! It's most definitely not a whale!"

The living spire flicked to and fro. Dubois turned in time to see it crash down across the stern of the *Ponce De Leon.*

-11-

White caps dotted the tops of the waves. The sea was beginning to look like a washing machine and Ray knew enough to be concerned. This was the kind of weather where you could easily get blindsided by a rogue wave. In a bigger boat, it wouldn't have concerned him as much. Hell, he'd navigated more than his share of storms, but this was different. Ray was in a lightweight, open body boat that could easily be swamped by a large enough wave.

The boat bounced across a set of close together waves and landed with a loud *thunk* on the water. Ray slowed his boat and turned a tight circle to head back and investigate. He should have been heading back towards Sunset Island, but what he would never admit is that he felt somewhat responsible for whatever had happened to that beardo, Alex. Sure, Ray wasn't *really* responsible. He had tried to tell that little idiot that what he wanted to do was a bad idea. It still bothered him. Ray could have warned Cal not to rent them a boat. Instead, he got drunk and stumbled home.

Ray hoped that he would find the Bayliner full of beardoes floating nearby with an empty gas tank. But it didn't look like hoping was amounting to much these days.

As Ray came around to check out whatever had thudded against the hull of his boat, he silently said a prayer that it would just be some trash and not a body. It wouldn't have been the first time someone from Sunset fished a bloated corpse out of the water. Morons, alcohol and water were always a dangerous mix. But Ray wasn't really in the mood to roll into town with a dead beardo or four in his boat.

"What's this shit?" Ray grumbled as he grabbed the trash out of the water. It was nothing of note, little more than a two-by-two blue square with ragged edges. The fact that the square was made of fiberglass and that the blue paint was exactly the kind used for painting the bottoms of boats is what bothered Ray. There was no way it was from Cal's Bayliner, but it was odd that he'd find it floating around where those idiots were heading.

A realization moved through Ray's head like cold honey across ice. He really should cut back on his drinking. No, not all of his drinking, just shots. Yeah, it was always those last few shots that packed his brain in cotton the next day. Ray shook his head and took in a deep breath of salty air as he scanned the area. Where the hell was the Glaxco rig?

More debris bobbed in the waves. Some of it had the Glaxco logo on it. The rest looked like part of a boat. Had those stupid ass beardoes crashed into the rig? No, it couldn't be that. Even if that was what Alex and his idiot friends had done, most of the rig should still be floating. Those things were built to take a lot more punishment than a run in with a fishing boat could dole out. And Ray was sure those Glaxco boys had been extra careful building this rig being that it was clouded in so much mystery.

Ray suddenly missed his rusty old ferry. It was the physical embodiment of everything he hated, but it was also large enough plow through the waves and it had a radio. His flat bottom clam boat was none of these things.

A cloudbank rolled across the horizon heading straight towards Sunset Island. It was damn near impossible to judge distance on the open water, but Ray could see the storm was closer than he'd have liked. At the base of the wall of clouds, something red and white stood out in stark contrast. Ray grabbed the binoculars that he kept looped over the steering wheel. No one ever really asked why Ray had binoculars on his clam boat and he was certainly in no rush to tell them. The truth was that not everything about them rich ladies was so terrible – evidently, a lot of money bought a little bikini. But none of that mattered at the moment. What mattered was that Ray was watching a large cargo freighter pitch backwards and split in half like the boat in that stupid as all hell Leonardo DiCaprio movie where the old broad chucks a diamond into the ocean. Ray remembered how angry Linda had been when they watched that movie and Ray expressed his disgust with the old lady. Why go through all that just to throw the damn necklace in the sea? Ray was sure her dead boyfriend would have much rather had her pawn the damn thing and live happily ever after. Linda scolded Ray for not being romantic and stormed off to the bedroom. Maybe the Big C liked that dumb movie.

Ray wondered why he was thinking about Linda so much lately. Maybe booze and waves had knocked some memories loose. Could he really miss her? She had been such a harsh and unpleasant woman towards the end, nothing like the beautiful girl he had fallen in love with in high school. Ray often marveled at pictures of the two of them from younger years. They had been so hopeful and marriage had drained them of it.

An icy spray of salt water shook Ray from his meandering down memory lane and he refocused on hauling ass to the cargo ship. Ray figured they must have come in to ride out the storm. Obviously, something had gone wrong with the plan. The ship couldn't be more than a few miles away, but those boys were in serious trouble. With no radio, Ray was left with few options. He gunned the engine and sped off towards the sinking ship.

Fuckin' hangover. I should'a gone to work today, Ray thought as his boat skipped across the waves like a stone.

-12-

Dubois had almost made it up the stairs on the side of the super structure when the *Ponce De Leon* pitched backwards. Dubois slipped on the metal stairs, grating skin from his knees.

"What is that thing?" Captain Bertrand shouted as he burst from the control room. A pistol was clutched in his trembling hand. Dubois had always thought the gun was ornamental, something to deter pirates and keep the crew in line. As the first shot cracked from the barrel, Dubois realized he had been mistaken.

"What are your orders, Captain?" Dubois asked, pulling himself up to standing. The thing that emerged from the water, a tentacle or a tail or some other ungodly appendage, had wrapped itself around the stern on the ship and was dragging it beneath the water. The ship groaned in protest as it began to break in half.

"Get the crew to the life boats, Mr. Dubois," Captain Bertrand shouted over his shoulder as he raced towards the thing destroying his ship. He fired shots from his pistol, but Dubois couldn't say if they hit their target or not. Even if the shots had hit the beast, they didn't appear to have any effect.

Dubois made the announcement to abandon ship, but most of the crew was already lowering lifeboats into the water. Dubois dashed down the stairs and leapt into the last lifeboat as three crewmembers turned the crank to lower it into the water. Five other boats bobbed below.

Captain Bertrand stood in the stern of the ship firing shots into the wall of sickly green that loomed before him. A ripple passed through the beast before it leapt into the air and crashed back down onto the deck. Captain Bertrand's pistol went silent.

The crew of the *Ponce De Leon* watched in a state of stupefied shock as their massive ship was torn in two and dragged beneath the waves. A loud hiss and spray of water filled the air as the air trapped inside the ship's two halves escaped.

"Come on then!" Dubois yelled to the crew. "Oars in the water! Start rowing for that island!" Dubois didn't know if the island he pointed at was Peach or Sunset and didn't care. All that he wanted to do was plant his feet on dry land and never set foot on a boat ever again.

Dubois and the three crewmembers rowed in the front, leading the other boats to safety. He couldn't help but stare back to the empty stretch of water where the *Ponce De Leon* had only moments ago floated. What creature possessed the strength to tear a cargo ship in two?

As if in answer to Dubois's silent question a swell of water rose behind the last lifeboat. A massive set of jaws rose around the small boat and pulled it beneath the waves. The crewmembers tried to leap to safety, but were swept up by the gaping mouth. A second lifeboat disappeared, then a third.

The men began to panic and strike the water with the oars. A large triangular form rose beneath one of the remaining lifeboats. The crewmembers lashed out with their oars, striking the creature before it rolled and flipped the boat. The men screamed and pleaded for help as they swam for the two remaining boats. One by one, they disappeared beneath the turbulent waves. Red froth rode between the waves.

Dubois grabbed the only remaining crewmember in the water and tried to pull him into the boat. The triangular form rose behind the man. A line appeared as the shape split in two revealing a tangled nest of dagger-like teeth. The mouth closed around the lower half of the man and pulled. Dubois held on the man's arms and tried to keep him in the boat. The lifeboat tipped and began taking on water. The other men leapt for the other side of the boat, violently wrenching Dubois in the opposite direction.

The man in Dubois's arms screamed and let out a plaintive cry. Dubois cradled the man's torso like a child as his innards spilled out across the bottom of the lifeboat. Dubois was covered by the sickening stew of blood, human waste and seawater that swirled about in the boat.

Dubois stared at the mangled remains in his lap. This had been a man only a few seconds ago. Now it was little more than a shredded wad of meat that stared at Dubois with glassy, lifeless eyes.

A loud splash and series of panicked screams echoed above the howling wind as the other lifeboat disappeared.

"Mr. Dubois!" one of the crewmembers shouted as he pulled him up from the bottom of the boat. "Mr. Dubois, what do we do now, sir?"

Dubois stared at the man. He could see his mouth moving, forming words and could see the emotion carved into the man's face, but had no idea what he was saying. Everything sounded muffled, lost in the wind.

The green spire broke the waves and pierced the stormy sky. Dubois thought he might have yelled or maybe pointed, but he couldn't be sure. The column of muscle flicked, throwing waves as it did, before crashing down onto the lifeboat.

Dubois was thrown into the air. He may have screamed, may have cursed this creature and whatever god had created it. He would never be sure. What Dubois was sure of was that a yellow eye, easily the height of a full-grown man, blinked at him from beneath the water before he slammed into an oncoming wave and everything went black.

-13-

"Holy shit!" Ray yelled above the wind as he watched the cargo ship break in half and sink beneath the waves. A few lifeboats dotted the sea. They weren't really more than simple rowboats, Ray thought. The boats were better suited for a pond than the middle of the ocean.

Then the lifeboats began to disappear. Men cried out for help. Ray already had the throttle opened up as wide as it would go and was already worried he might flip the boat.

Ray watched something tall and pointed rise out of the waves. It looked black against the gray sky, but he was pretty sure he saw what looked like spikes running along side. It flicked back and forth before crashing down onto the remaining lifeboat. The silhouette of a man's body was launched from the bow of the lifeboat and consumed by an approaching wave. Whatever had emerged from the water disappeared again below.

The large seventy-five-horse power Mercury growled as it pushed the boat forward and cut through the waves. Spray leapt from the sides and bow throwing salt into Ray's eyes. He squinted and blinked, but kept his hands firmly on the steering wheel.

The man's body bobbed in the waves facedown. Ray pulled the throttle back and grabbed him by the collar of his uniform. Whatever had attacked the cargo ship was still around, but Ray forced himself to focus on nothing but saving the man. As the man landed in the bottom of the boat, Ray couldn't help but think of a marlin he had reeled in years ago. It had taken hours to bring the fish aboard. Once Ray had, he felt compelled to throw it back. The fish was a fighter, much like Ray saw himself, and had won its right to exist.

The man coughed and vomited salty water all over himself and the boat. Ray slapped his back.

"Come on now," Ray said, "out with all that. Spit it out so ya can breathe." The man coughed a few more times. His eyes were wide and shot with blood.

A scream the likes of which Ray had never heard tore from the man's throat. His trembling hand curled back and he pointed his finger towards the sea.

A wall of water rose from the sea and moved towards Ray's boat in a wide curving path. He scrambled over the bench and fumbled with the controls. The boat roared with mechanical glee as Ray pushed it further.

Ray whipped the wheel and turned the boat towards Peach Island. He wanted nothing more than to be home on Sunset. No, he didn't want to be at home. Where he wanted to be was at The Dry Dock drunkenly teetering on a stool while Big Mo told dirty jokes and served flat beer. Ray would have given anything to be safely within the sticky bosom of The Dry Dock, but that wasn't going to happen.

What was going to happen was that Ray was going to get himself, his boat and the screaming man to Peach Island before whatever had sunk the cargo ship did the same to his little clam boat.

Ray had saltwater flowing through his veins. He was a third generation fisherman and could name just about any creature that swam the waters surrounding Sunset Island. But what he had seen rise from the water and smash the lifeboat was strange and unknown. No whale or shark moved like that. And no octopus or squid was that large. Ray had heard drunken tales of giant squids, but those were supposed to be out in the Pacific somewhere, not in the waters around Sunset.

A curved ridge that shone like polished jade broke the sea. It was dotted with a series of small brown horns. A yellow eye with a triangular black iris glared at Ray as it rose above the turbulent waves. This was no squid.

Now it was Ray's turn to scream.

-14-

The weather was a total bitch today. There was supposed to be a kick ass barbeque going on. People were supposed to be drinking dark rum and posing for kick ass pictures in the ruins of a secret government laboratory. The pictures would be epic on Instagram, especially with the new filters just downloaded from the App Store.

As it was, there were no pictures worth taking. Who wanted to see a bunch of people in drenched, albeit fashionable clothes, huddled into tents complaining about the weather? There was nothing worth posting a picture of today. No one online was going to be jealous of this.

"My swimsuit is totally chaffing my ass," Georgie groaned. He pulled at the red and white striped fabric.

"I told you that sand would get caught in there," Nicola laughed. "Told you people stopped wearing those for a reason."

"But it looks so cool," Georgie shrugged.

"What'd that old dude want?" Nicola asked.

"Looking for his boyfriend or something," Georgie snickered. "Said something about a storm too. I don't really remember. I was still tweaked from last night."

"A storm?" Nicola's well-practiced mask of disdain for the mundane faltered. Georgie was fun and his dad's bank account ensured that the fun never stopped, but Georgie didn't know his ass from his elbow when it came to camping. Not that it really mattered when the sun was shining and the rum was flowing, but now with a storm rolling in, Nicola was worried.

"Just a little rain, girl, that's all," Georgie grinned. "Jeez, you know how those dumb yokels are. Like his knee hurts or something, and he's gotta run down the street yelling about the storm to end all storms. It's just a little summer rain." Nicola laughed, but it was cut short by a deafening thunderclap. The tent shook as the wind tried to pull the stakes from the sandy ground.

Somewhere in the distance, Nicola could have sworn she heard yelling and the roar of a boat engine, but couldn't really be sure. "Maybe we should see if other people are packing up. Might be able to catch a ride off the island." She and Georgie had paddled over in a rented kayak, a rented kayak that a drunken Georgie had managed to flip and sink. Nicola thought some genius Eskimo scientist had designed those things to be unsinkable. Evidently, Georgie had found a way.

Georgie made a rude noise and waved his hand. "I'm not going anywhere. This tent is totally fine, babe. It had a ton of five star reviews on Amazon, so it's totally fine."

"Yeah, maybe," Nicola agreed. "But still, I think I heard a boat. I'm just going to go and check."

"Whatever makes you smile, girl," Georgie lay back on his sleeping bag.

The wind whipped at Nicola's straw colored hair as the rain tried to paste it to the side of her head. She squinted and tried to find where the other tents were set up. It looked like everyone had packed up, but with the rain coming sideways, it was damn near impossible to say. Nicola was pretty sure she could trip over a tent or passed out partier with her next step. She kind of hoped that she would.

The ground rumbled beneath Nicola's feet. At first, it was little more than a gentle twitch, the sand lightly tickling her feet. Could have been anything or nothing at all. Maybe just a distance bit of thunder. Nicola checked the sky for lightning. A few bolts of blinding purple cut across the sky and struck the horizon. The ground shook again. *When had the sky gotten so dark?* Nicola wondered. *Uh, duh! The storm!* She laughed at her own stupidity, but couldn't shake the feeling that the sky looked darker than it should have been.

Well, it looked like everyone else had shipped out and Nicola was going to have to ride the storm out in Georgie's smelly tent. But where was the tent? And where the hell was Georgie? Nicola squinted as a gust of wind blasted her in the face. The rain was cold and felt like it cut her skin. She rubbed her face and tried to remember where Georgie had set up his stupid tent.

"Whoa, shit!" Nicola cried as she fell face first into the wet sand. "What the hell? When was there a hole here?" She rolled over and pushed herself up to sitting. Something hard brushed against the side of her hand. Nicola grabbed the object and brought it closer. It felt like a stick or something. Lightning flashed and Nicola caught a glimpse of what she held. It was tent stake. But there could be a million tent stakes left here by other campers. It didn't mean it was Georgie's tent stake. But wasn't this where they had set up the tent?

"Georgie? Georgie, where are you? Stop screwing around, Georgie! This isn't funny!" Nicola yelled over the wind. A shadow thudded to the ground behind her. Nicola spun around to see what it was. A wet chunk of meat lay in the sand. It was stringy and looked chewed. Scraps of red and white fabric were tangled around the meat and whipped in the wind.

"Georgie?" Nicola stammered. A wall of black loomed over her, blocking out the stormy sky. Nicola couldn't tell what it was, couldn't put a name to the nightmare that stood over her, but could see that it was chewing. It was definitely chewing.

The ground shook as the creature shifted. An involuntary scream tore from Nicola's throat. Lightning flashed and a colossal yellow eye glared down at her. Nicola turned and ran. The sand trembled beneath her bare feet. The rain and wind lashed at her face.

The remains of the government buildings peeked out from behind the trees. Nicola didn't know what this thing would do if it caught her, but she sure as hell wasn't going to wait around on the beach to find out. She ducked inside what was left of an old two story concrete building.

The structure was little more than four gray walls. The windows were long gone and a tree had broken through the roof. Garbage from countless parties littered the ground. Nicola pressed herself against the far wall and prayed that whatever was outside would leave. She trembled, her teeth were chattering, but it had nothing to do with the cold rain or wind.

The building shook and concrete fell from the ceiling. The tree in the center of the room splintered and was gone. Another trunk stood in its place. This one was four times as wide and covered with a gnarly black bark. Nicola had been all over Peach Island the last few days and had never come across a tree that looked like this one. The storm was strong, but was it really strong enough to have uprooted a tree of this size and dropped it through the roof of a building?

The roots at the base of the tree writhed and shifted. One shot towards Nicola. Something warm ran down her bare stomach. How had tree had speared her through the stomach? Nicola's hands tenderly touched her stomach. They came back warm and sticky.

Nicola coughed, throwing a dark spray of blood across the talon that speared her. She tried to break free from the creature's hold, but the remaining claws closed around her. Nicola disappeared through the hole in the roof. Her screams, though short lived, were lost in the howling winds.

-15-

Ray did a quick lap around Peach Island. He wished the man in his boat would be more useful, but after screaming his lungs out, he passed out and was now slumped against a bench. Had the man been awake, Ray would have told him to blast the air horn a few times and get the attention of whatever beardoes were stupid enough to still be on Peach Island. As it was, Ray settled for screaming and waving his arms, not that it mattered.

None of the beardoes was on the beach. A few tents dotted the island and a couple of boats, but no one was outside and there was no way they were going to hear Ray over the storm winds and the roar of his boat's engines. He had tried to warn these idiots, had told them to pack up and leave, but they didn't listen. They were a bunch of over privileged know it alls, but that didn't mean that Ray wanted to see them get hurt.

Whatever had sunk the cargo ship and killed most of its crew was still in the water behind Ray's boat. It moved like a snake in wide sweeping zigzags that cut through waves with each motion. Ray had caught a glimpse of some of it, but his mind still struggled to piece together what creature was capable of the carnage he had just witnessed.

Ray needed to haul ass back to Sunset Island and warn everyone. They would probably think he was drunk or crazy, but a bloodstained sailor would go a long way in terms of credibility and evidence. Hopefully, most of the boats around Sunset Island had heeded the hurricane warning and gone into port. Most people should be safe, so long as they stayed on dry land. Or at least that's what Ray hoped.

Whatever was trailing his boat, Ray hoped that it was purely aquatic. He wanted that thing to stay in the water, not only for the sake of those dumb ass beardoes, but for the sake of everyone on Sunset Island as well. A giant monster in the water was one thing. One on land was another nightmare entirely.

The dim flame of hope that Ray fanned fluttered and went out when he looked over his shoulder and saw the creature turn towards Peach Island. It slowed as it reached the shallow water near the beach. Ray couldn't see many details, but the shadowy outline told him more than enough.

Jagged spikes broke the water, followed by a massive serpentine body. The back was curved upwards and ridged with spikes. A set of large muscular shoulders lifted a broad triangular head above the waves. Four legs, the width of tree trunks, stepped over the storm waves as if they were nothing more than ripples on a puddle. A thick tail lifted out of the water and swept back and forth through the stormy sky. With one step, the monster was on dry land and moving towards a cluster of beardo tents.

"Holy mother Mary," Ray mumbled. He could have sworn he was watching a late night monster movie, but the cold rain on his face let him know this was real. He was really watching a monster emerge from the sea and lumber onto Peach Island. Still, his mind struggled to fit these pieces together. This kind of shit wasn't supposed to happen around here. Well, it wasn't supposed to happen *anywhere*, but most certainly not around here. This was something for the Japanese, with their leaky nuclear power plants and love affair with giant monsters to worry about. But it sure as hell was not supposed to be swimming around in Ray's backyard. He had never seen anything larger than a shark or a marlin in these parts. Sure, once in a while you could spot a whale, but nothing like this.

There was nothing Ray could do. He slowed the boat. A silent prayer was uttered for those kids, but with the next flash of lightning, Ray saw that God either wasn't listening or didn't care.

The monster closed its massive jaws around a tent and lifted it high into the air. Even from this distance, Ray could see it chewing. He really wished those stupid kids had listened.

But none of that mattered now. All that Ray could do was get to Sunset and warn everyone. But what was he going to tell them? What kind of plan did a little vacation destination have when fucking Godzilla showed up? Ray hoped they had a good one, because he was going to be asking about it soon enough.

Ray gunned the engine and turned towards Sunset Island.

-16-

Mayor Billings looked across the small gathering of people in front of him. The high school auditorium should be full, what with all the ferry folk and all, but for the most part, all Billings saw was locals. He had called this meeting in response to the hurricane warning and to assure the vacationers that everything was going to be just fine. There was no reason to panic. No reason to leave and take all of their wonderful money with them. No, everything on Sunset Island would be just fine.

Fighting his gut, Mayor Billings pulled his pants up authoritatively and walked towards the podium. He could feel the hot stage lights blasting down onto his bald spot and wished that his comb-over were doing a better job of protecting it.

Clearing his throat, Mayor Billings smiled out at the crowd. There were maybe fifty people here, not nearly was many as he had the janitor set up chairs for. Every empty folding chair was like a four-legged middle finger waggling in Mayor Billings' face.

"Good people of Sunset Island and our treasured summer friends," Mayor Billings began.

"Don't you mean our *summer friend's treasure?*" some shouted from the rear of the auditorium. The crowd began laughing and banging on their seats. Mayor Billings could feel his anger washing across his back in hot waves. Sweat prickled his forehead and began to streak down his thick neck and catch in the large rolls of glistening flesh. Mayor Billings couldn't be sure who said it, but as his eyes settled on Big Mo. He felt confident she'd been the culprit. That sea hag and her drunken cronies, especially Ray, were a constant thorn in Billings' considerable ass. Speaking of the liquor soaked ferryboat Captain, where the hell was he?

"Everything is going to be just fine," Mayor Billings continued. "I have checked the weather maps and feel confident that we have nothing to worry about. Sunset Island is going to be just fine."

"Then why the hell is there a line of cars for three blocks waiting to get off the island?" another townie loser catcalled from the back.

"Shit," Mayor Billings mumbled, regretting that he was standing close to the microphone. If the summer people were abandoning the island it could ruin the entire vacation season and Billings couldn't stomach the idea of all that money going somewhere else. On the other hand, forcing them to stay could be equally as dangerous. The last thing Mayor Billings needed was some pissed off city dweller writing a nasty review online. He had worked hard to drag Sunset Island into the same echelon as the Hamptons. It was basic math. He could lose a little money this season or all of it the next.

"What was that, Mayor?" Big Mo cackled. "Couldn't hear you? Can you run that one by us again?"

"As always, Mo, your concern and insight are appreciated," Mayor Billings smiled. "Has anyone seen Ray?" No one answered. "Big Mo, did you check the floor of that shit hole you call a bar?"

"Mayor, you know we filled in the shit hole after the health inspector told us to," Big Mo laughed. "I could always dig it out if you were looking for a snack."

Mayor Billings ignored Big Mo's offer. "Jimmy? Jimmy, are you here?"

"Right here, Mayor," Jimmy waved half-heartedly.

"Great," Mayor Billings nodded. "And might I ask why you're here instead of on the ferry shuttling those people to safety?"

"Mayor," Jimmy said, "National Hurricane Center said that all boats should remain in port. I don't really think it's a good idea."

"Fortunately, you're not the one who gets paid to think," Mayor Billings seethed. "What is it? Just a few miles between Sunset and the mainland? Jimmy, stop being such a pain in the ass and get that ferry moving."

"Don't you think it'd be better to have Ray do it?" Big Mo chimed in. "No offense, Jim. I love ya, but if anyone's gonna drive the ferry through the middle of a damn hurricane, shouldn't it be the Captain?"

"Shit, none taken," Jimmy laughed. "I'm just glad someone else said it before I had to. I gotta say, Mayor, I think Big Mo is right. If anyone is going to navigate the storm it should be Ray."

"What a wonderful idea," Mayor Billings spat. "Let's have the drunken sea captain, who is conveniently missing, pilot a damn ferry loaded down with all of Sunset's tourist! No! Shut up and go get that damn ferry moving!"

Jimmy looked around the crowd. The most support anyone appeared to be willing to offer was a shrug. Jimmy stood up and shuffled towards the door.

Mayor Billings droned on for a few more minutes after Jimmy had left for the ferry. Most of the crowd remained silent. Maybe they were worried about Jimmy. Maybe they had rubbed their beer soaked brain cells together too many times and run out of witty things to shout. Either way, Mayor Billings didn't care.

The rear door of the auditorium banged open and rattled against the wall as the wind repeatedly smashed it back. Rain blew in through the open door, soaking the floor.

"Jimmy, you dumb son of a bitch," Mayor Billings shouted. "I told you to get your stupid ass to the ferry!"

"You told him to what?" Ray growled. He had the arm of some unknown man in a khaki uniform around his shoulder. Dark stains were spattered across the man's uniform.

"No time to get into a pissing contest over the captain's chair, Ray," Mayor Billings laughed. "You were off doing something else, so I sent Jimmy."

"You sent Jimmy to his fuckin' death, you asshole," Ray shouted.

"Jeez, Ray, whatever you've been drinking at The Dry Dock must've been damn strong. There's no need to be so dramatic about a little storm," Mayor Billings laughed.

"I ain't talking about the damn storm, you bastard," Ray paused and looked at his friends and neighbors. "I'm talking about the damn monster."

-17-

Jimmy's breath kept fogging up the windows on the ferry, not that it really mattered. The rain was coming down hard and the wipers weren't doing much against it.

"Dumb, dumb, dumb," Jimmy grumbled as he used his sleeve to wipe the window. He wasn't sure if he was talking about the Mayor, the storm or himself. Maybe it was all three. Jimmy had already decided he wasn't making the return trip. No sir, the ferry was staying safely docked on the mainland side until this storm rolled out to sea.

The ferry was loaded down with cars and ferry folk, which wasn't making it any easier to navigate the waves that smashed against the boat. The waves were coming over the sides of the ferry and coating all those fancy cars with salt. At least it was also keeping all the ferry folk locked inside their cars.

"Man, oh, man," Jimmy muttered as he turned the ferry to avoid a set of large waves. The boat pitched sideways, but stayed the course. "We got no business being out in this. None. Shit. Where the fuck was Ray anyway? He's the only one that should be out in this storm. I got no business out here."

The ferry groaned and shuddered. Jimmy stumbled forward and banged his stomach against the control panel. A few car alarms wailed down on the deck. The ferry must have hit something, but what? There weren't any sandbars out this far. But what else could stop a ferry at full steam? Even if Jimmy had hit another boat, it wouldn't have stopped the ferry, not unless it was huge. The visibility was total shit, but Jimmy was certain he hadn't rammed another boat.

A few people shouted from their cars.

"Shut up and stay in your damn cars!" Jimmy shouted over the wind. A couple of deckhands peered over the front of the ferry. They were barely visible through the rain and sea spray.

A loud cry echoed from the bow of the boat. Jimmy couldn't tell which of the crewmembers were investigating, but he could see there was now one less.

"Man overboard! Man overboard!" Jimmy screamed. He rushed back into the control room and sounded the alarm. Crewmembers rushed outside in yellow slickers, the rain glistening under the sodium floodlights set high above the deck. Everything was orange or black, like some hellish Halloween party. Occasionally, a bright flash of lightning would streak across the sky, but did little to change the mood.

"What's going on? Why did we stop?" a guy in a SUV shouted. Jimmy looked at the upturned collar on the guy's polo shirt and wanted to punch him in the face.

"Sir, get back in your car," Jimmy snapped.

"We can't just float around out here," Polo Shirt argued. "Get back up there and drive the boat!" Mrs. Polo Shirt shouted from inside the SUV, cheering her husband on.

Jimmy had shoved Polo Shirt against the side of his car before he even realized what he was doing. He leaned in, bringing his face within millimeters of the other man's. "Get. The. Fuck. In. Your. Car. Now!" Polo Shirt's eyes went wide and he silently slipped back into his SUV.

A second scream cut through the night. Another crewmember was gone. Jimmy turned and rushed towards the front of the ferry. All of the crewmembers were gone.

"Captain, something grabbed them!" a little boy yelled from a nearby car.

"I'm not the Captain, kid," Jimmy said. "What'd you mean *something grabbed them?*"

"I saw it," the kid continued. "It came out of the water and grabbed them!"

"Kid, I got no time for this," Jimmy turned back towards the water. There should be strobes flashing. The lights went off automatically when they hit the water and all the crew had them on their jackets. The waves were dark.

The ferry pitched forward. Jimmy expected to see the face of a massive wave bearing down on them. He certainly didn't expect to see a monstrous claw, tipped in four talons clamped onto the front of the boat.

"There it is!" the kid shouted. He pointed.

Jimmy wanted to tell the kid to run. To get the kid and his parents to climb into a lifeboat, but there were none. There was nowhere to run. The ferry was never meant to be out in a storm like this and sure as hell wasn't supposed to have a living nightmare climbing onto the front of it.

Cars slipped on the wet deck and slid towards Jimmy. He could jump over the side of the ferry and face the monster or stay on the deck and get crushed. He chose something in the middle.

Jimmy had loved dinosaurs as a kid. His parents had filled the shelves of his bedroom with books and models. Maybe if he had lived somewhere else he would have become a paleontologist or something like that?

At the present moment, Jimmy hated every reptile with every single fiber of his being, especially the one that loomed over the ferry.

Pain exploded in Jimmy's back as Polo Shirt's SUV slammed him to the deck. Salt water rushed over the front of the ferry. Jimmy coughed seawater and blood onto the deck.

A deafening roar thundered above the storm as the ferry was dragged beneath the waves.

-18-

Mayor Billings was a Grade A moron. Ray had known that before he sent Jimmy out into a hurricane with a ferry full of summer tourists. Now Ray could see that had been a complete understatement. Once he saved Jimmy's ass, he was going to skin Billings.

The rain streaked down Ray's face and the wind ripped at this sodden clothes.

"We're going back out there?" the man in the khaki uniform asked.

"Mister, I don't even know your name, so I don't see how I can ask you to go back out there with that monster and all." Ray untied the bow of his clam boat and tossed the coil of rope into the bow.

"My name is Dubois and thanks for saving me. Now that we've cleared that up, let's go." Dubois untied the remaining line and leapt off the dock into the boat.

"Guess that settles it," Ray shrugged and started up the engine. "So what happened out there? I mean other than the obvious."

Dubois moved over the bench nearest the steering wheel. "Not really sure about that one. I was second in command on the *Ponce De Leon.* We were a cargo freighter making our way north from Haiti. When we heard the hurricane warning, I talked Captain Bertrand into bringing the ship closer to land to ride out the storm." Dubois let his words hang in the air like a noose.

"Ain't your fault," Ray yelled over the wind. He scanned the waves for any sign of the ferry. "You just did what any sailor with half a brain would'a done. Ain't no way you could know there was a fucking sea monster swimming around these parts."

"You really think it's a sea monster?" Dubois asked.

"You got a better name for that thing?" Ray answered. "Cuz it sure as all hell looked like a sea monster to me."

"Agreed," Dubois nodded as he remembered the monster tearing the *Ponce De Leon* apart. The screams of his crew being pulled beneath the water echoed through his head. "I guess something that could do that is definitely a monster. But I've spent most of my life on or near the water and have never seen anything like that. Nothing with a tentacle that could rip a ship in half."

"Wasn't no tentacle, Dubois," Ray shook his head. "What you saw was a tail."

"A tail?" Dubois shouted over the wind and engine.

"Yup," Ray answered. "When you was passed out, I saw the creature come up outta the water and climb up onto Peach Island. Them kids camping out there ain't never had a chance. No sir, that was not tentacle. It was a tail on the ass of a giant monster."

"What'd the rest of it look like?" Dubois asked. He didn't really want to know what the nightmare that killed his crew looked like, but not knowing was worse. He needed to know what they were up against.

"Kind of like a giant lizard, I guess," Ray answered. He paused and then continued. "Exactly like that."

Ray pointed off the bow of the boat. A hulking lizard climbed over the sinking remains of the ferry.

"Well, guess that settles that," Ray growled as he watched the ferry sink. No strobes bobbed in the waves. No one cried out for help. All those people were dead. Jimmy was dead.

"What now?" Dubois asked. The monster crunched a section of rusted metal between its jaws. It stopped, spit the metal into the waves and turned towards the small clam boat. The same yellow eyes that had glared at Dubois from beneath the water once again bore into him.

"Now?" Ray swung the wheel hard to left and turned the back towards Sunset Island. "Now we get the fuck out of here."

A loud splash rippled across the water behind the small clam boat.

"Sounds like the best idea I've ever heard!" Dubois screamed over the roaring wind.

-19-

"Everyone, please remain calm," Mayor Billings yelled over the clamor of the crowd. The townsfolk had been joined by the remaining ferry folk who grew tired of waiting for the ferry to return. It left with a full load of cars, but never returned. "I assure you good people that the ferry will return and that we will get you safely off the island. But for the time being, please just remain calm."

"The fucking ferry isn't coming back, you lying sack of shit!" Big Mo shouted.

How come the stupid ones are always louder than the rest? Mayor Billings wondered as he glared at Big Mo. People were beginning to panic.

"Now listen," Mayor Billings smashed his hammy fist on the podium. "We've heard enough about sea monsters and stupidity alike, so let's just shelve that lunacy and remain safe and warm right here. As soon as Jimmy is back with the ferry, he will sound the horn and if you still want a ride to the mainland, I'll personally make sure you get one. But for the time being, the best thing we can do is sit tight."

The lights flickered three times. People gasped, but the lights stayed on. The lights flickered again, but this time stayed out. People began to shout.

"That's enough!" Big Mo's voice boomed over the crowd. In the dim red glow of the school's emergency lights, Mayor Billings could see the sizable bartender standing on a folding chair. "Enough with this idiot and his plans. Everybody, just calm the fuck down. The Dry Dock is right around the corner and we've got a generator, so that means warm asses and cold beers. Anyone wants to join me, that's where I'll be and y'all are welcome to join."

"Them and their money, I bet," Mayor Billings laughed.

"Hey, Mayor," Big Mo called from the doorway, "fuck you, fuck your plans and fuck this. You know damn well that hurricane rules are different. Anyone in The Dry Dock is drinking for free so long as this storm is blowing. We take care of each other around here. Or at least most of us do."

Mayor Billings' mouth hung open, his jowls trembling with rage. A large portion of people moved to follow Big Mo to The Dry Dock. Even a handful of ferry folk shuffled alongside the townies.

"Let them go," Mayor Billings waved his thick hand dismissively. "We'll be just fine. You good, intelligent folks have my word. Yes, sir, everything is going to be just fine."

-20-

The water was already higher. When Ray untied his clam boat to go search for that little beardo moron in Cal's Bayliner, he had to jump down from the dock. Now the boat and dock were almost even.

"We gotta move," Ray shouted over his shoulder. Dubois was busy tying off the lines – some habits refused to die. "Just leave the damn boat, Dubois. Storm is gonna wreck the dock anyway. Come on."

Dubois dropped the line and followed Ray off the dock. All of Sunset was dark. The flicker of a few candles could be seen behind storm shutters, but for the most part the island looked deserted. Small rivers streamed down the streets and pooled in the intersections where the storm drains were clogged with debris and sand.

"Where is everyone?" Dubois asked as he caught up to Ray. The salty Captain looked old, but moved with purpose and strength.

"Most of 'em are probably still down at the high school, would be my guess," Ray pointed behind them.

"Wait?" Dubois stopped. His khaki uniform had turned from a light tan to almost black from the endless rain. "If the high school is back that way, then why are we going this way?"

"Cause the high school was built on low land and only an idiot would hole up there during a hurricane. Besides, this way leads to The Dry Dock," Ray kept walking.

"What is The Dry Dock? Why are we going there?" Dubois questioned. He followed Ray around the corner and up a small hill. A small clapboard building with a rowboat on the top loomed over them. The neon lights glowing in the foggy windows looked warm and inviting.

"That's The Dry Dock," Ray answered. "And we're going to The Dry Dock cuz they have a generator and are on top of a hill. Besides, be honest, Dubois. It's already been a shit day and it's only gonna get worse. Way I figure it, you and me, we both earned a couple of drinks before the fucking sea monster shows up."

Dubois thought about arguing, but the idea of a few moments of warmth and reprieve from the nightmare that was his life was too tempting.

"I'm buying the first round," Dubois said.

"Shit, son," Ray laughed as he held the door to the bar open. "You definitely ain't from around here. There's a hurricane blowing. That means everyone drinks for free."

-21-

Carson was alone in his family's summer home. It was huge and felt empty, even when the rest of the Creswell family was in it. Now though, it was actually empty. Carson's dad had taken the ferry back to the mainland early in the morning. He said that he had to work, but Carson knew it had more to do with the loud fight he heard in the middle of the night between his mom and dad. His mom had done her usual, left a cold breakfast, half-hearted note and disappeared to the yacht club. Carson's brother and sister were somewhere, probably a bar, probably drunk, but definitely not home. As it would seem, each member of the Creswell family assumed one of the others would be looking after young Carson, which no one was.

The wind howled outside of Carson's house and he could see the waves smashing against the retaining wall. It wouldn't be long before the waves got over the wall and spilled into the street. Carson hoped his family was safe, even if the notion wasn't returned.

Carson had been on Sunset Island a few summers ago when another storm had blown in. His father was excited to shutter the windows and organize all his tools and supplies. Granted, the storm hadn't really been anything more than some rain and a little bit of wind, but Carson had felt safe when his dad closed up the house.

Running up to the second floor, Carson watched the storm from the large sliding glass doors that led to the balcony off his parents' bedroom. It probably would have been more accurate to say his mother's bedroom, since she slept here and Carson's dad usually 'fell asleep watching TV on the couch' but Carson wasn't in the mood to think about these things. There were more important things to worry about. With everyone gone, he was the man of the house. And being the man of the house meant making sure the house was safe.

The wind threatened to toss Carson's small form off the side of the balcony, but he gripped the railing tight and made his way over to release the storm shutters. Slowly, with stinging rain pelting his face and arms, Carson dropped the storm shutters.

After the shutters were securely in place Carson cast a quick glance down to the beach, or at least the little strip of sand that had yet to be consumed by the waves. It was scary to see dark swells of water battering the beach and to hear the deafening roar as they broke against the sea wall. Still, Carson looked down onto the beach. The storm was scary, but still the big waves would pull the sharks and dolphins back out to sea where they belonged, so it couldn't be all bad.

A wave, this one larger and faster than the others, moved towards Carson's house. He watched wide-eyed as the wave overtook smaller ones and moved past them. This wave was definitely going to crash over the sea wall. Carson worried it might swallow his house.

A thunderous sound resonated over the wailing winds. The dark water parted like stage curtains and rained onto the sand. In place of the wave stood a terrifying image.

Carson, like all kids, had shared an obligatory love affair with dinosaurs at one point in his life. But dinosaurs had eventually lost out to sea creatures. Still Carson could remember and name most dinosaurs by picture alone. What stood before Carson had never been illustrated in one of his dinosaur books. No, this was not a dinosaur. This was a monster.

The monster silently crept onto the beach, its large, heavily muscled legs holding in close to the ground. It was on the sea wall in less than two steps, gripping the logs between its claws like they were little more than toothpicks.

Carson wanted to run and scream. He wanted to wake up. He wanted his parents. The freezing rain kept Carson present in the moment. The warm urine running down his leg let him know this was real.

A yellow eye with a black diamond shaped iris examined Carson from the other side of the balcony railing. Small spiky horns ringed the monster's eye. A pair of scaly nostrils sniffed the air as a forked tongue the length of Carson darted in and out of the monster's awful looking mouth. Rain pooled on the monster's scaly, jagged skin and spilled down the sides of the massive beast.

Carson remained frozen in place, his own terrified image reflected in the monster's humongous eye. The creature grunted and sniffed the air. Something seemed to draw its attention towards the center of Sunset. It turned away from Carson's house, crushing Mr. Van Bolden's expensive car beneath its clawed feet.

Carson's lungs burned like fire and he realized he had been holding his breath. Whatever that thing was, Carson was glad to see it go and even happier that no one had been home to tease him for wetting his pants. Still, Carson felt pretty sure that peeing your pants was allowed when you were staring at a monster. Even his mean older brother couldn't argue a fact like that.

Carson exhaled and tried to relax. He had done well. He was the man of the house and he had kept it safe from a storm *and* a monster. Carson watched the monster pass between his house and Mr. Van Bolden's house. Mr. Van Bolden would be sad about his car, but Carson was sure some wrestling with the yacht club waitress would change all that. Carson turned to watch the monster move towards town, worried for everyone else, but happy that he was safe. He turned and never saw the monster's tail, ridged with spikes, sweeping towards the balcony.

-22-

Like most situations, time and waiting had made even the hurricane boring. Mayor Billings had a gift for manipulating situations and seeing the long game, but small town success had cursed him with a sense of instant gratification. He had saved his people and led them, but now what? The power was out. The wind was howling. And worst of all Mayor Billings was bored.

A few people gathered around a propane lantern and battered Monopoly board.

"Want to play, Mayor?" One of the players offered him the thimble.

"No, no," Mayor Billings smiled. "Let one of the children have my place. Make sure they are occupied." The truth was that Mayor Billings felt engaged in a perpetual game of Monopoly where Sunset Island was the board. Playing it on the small scale would have been no distraction at all. Billings would have liked to have thought of himself as the racecar or classy top hat, but the truth was his shape lent itself more to the thimble. And on most days, he felt like that old boot or the backside of the horse. But who cares? That was the genius of monopoly, right? You could be the thimble or old boot and still own Park Place and Boardwalk.

The words of Big Mo were irksome, but little more. Let her take the drunks and troublemakers to her shitty old bar. Who needed them anyway? Mayor Billings was left with the good people of Sunset and a few ferry folk. That was much more preferable to a room packed full of morons and alcoholics.

The heavy metal doors leading into the auditorium crashed open and people screamed as their candles were snuffed out by the gusting storm winds. The lantern near the Monopoly board cast a flickering amber light, just enough for Mayor Billings to see water spilling through the doors.

"Everyone, please remain calm," Mayor Billings raised his hands. "It appears there is a storm surge and flooding. We are still safe. Please gather your things."

"Gather our things?" someone shouted from the darkness. "Where are you going to lead us now, Moses? Down to the beach club maybe?"

Mayor Billings swallowed his anger. "No, we will not be going to the *beach club*. We are moving to higher ground where we will be safe."

"Higher ground?" one of the panicked shadows asked. "Like at The Dry Dock?"

"Absolutely not," Mayor Billings snapped. "We will not be taking children to that sleazy place. We will leave the school and follow Poplar Street to the church. The church is on high ground and has a raised foundation. We will be fine there."

"Then why didn't we go there in the first place?" some demanded.

"Unless you have the plans for a time machine, I suggest you get your things and follow me to the church," Mayor Billings shouted at the shadows around him.

"Screw this. I'm going to The Dry Dock, like we should've in the first place," a man yelled from the doorway.

"Then go!" Mayor Billings screamed. "You can go to Hell for all I care!"

The man turned to give the mayor the middle finger, and succeeded in almost doing so before he was snapped off the ground and lifted high into the air. His screams swirled with the storm winds to create a terrifying banshee's wail.

Organs and chunks of ragged meat splattered on the sidewalk outside the high school auditorium. People began to scream again.

"What was that?" someone demanded. "Mayor, what the hell was that?"

Mayor Billings could feel all eyes in the auditorium fixed on him. These people were terrified. Truth be told, Mayor Billings was terrified. But his position demanded leadership and answers, even if the mayor didn't really have any to offer.

"It must have been a tree or something of that nature," Mayor Billings muttered. "Yes, that's it. I believe that poor man must have been killed by a falling tree or perhaps some debris that had been caught up in the winds."

"Trees don't have fucking teeth!" someone yelled. "He was eaten!"

"Eaten?" Mayor Billings scoffed. "What on earth could have possibly eaten a full grown adult male in one bite. Do not let your boredom and hysteria get the better of you. No, a falling tree injured that poor man. That is all. If you believe otherwise, well I'd say you're welcome to go outside and investigate. But I'll be staying here until I think it is safe to move to the church."

Murmurs of disagreement rippled through the crowd. People shuffled in the darkness, but no one openly argued. Mayor Billings' explanation had been thin, but no volunteers were quick to go outside and offer a different one.

"What about the water?" some asked.

Mayor Billings looked down. The water had risen another three inches in the time they had been arguing.

"Gather your things," Mayor Billings said with all the authority he could muster. "We are moving to the church."

Leadership and answers. That was what Mayor Billings was paid to do.

-23-

People were packed into The Dry Dock, but as soon as Ray walked through the door, someone stood up to give him a stool at the bar. Dubois could see that the people around here respected Ray, even if it didn't appear that he respected himself.

"What're you drinking?" a mountain of a woman with a shock of red hair asked.

"Whiskey, please, Big Mo." Ray motioned towards Dubois.

"Yeah, whiskey would be fine. Thanks," Dubois said. He swiveled on his bar stool and took the bar. A few of the people looked out of place. The rest looked like locals. All looked drunk.

"Here you go," Big Mo placed two glasses of whiskey in front of the men. Dubois noticed she had nearly filled both. "Looks like you had a rough night out there." Big Mo smiled and pointed towards the glasses of liquor.

"Thanks," Dubois nodded and drained half of the glass. Ray nodded his approval and did the same.

"So, Ray, um…well look," Big Mo said. "Some people been talking bout what you said back there at the high school. Most think you were out drinking or hit your head or something, but I known you my whole life and ain't never known you to make shit up, no matter how much booze you got movin' through your veins."

Ray emptied his whiskey glass. "Can I get another one, Big Mo? Please?" She picked up the glass, filled it, but wouldn't hand it back to Ray. "Thanks."

"So would you care to tell me what the hell happened out there, Ray?" Big Mo held the glass of whiskey out of his reach.

"Jeez, Mo," Ray groaned. "I ain't even drunk yet. Couldn't you at least wait until my clothes dried out and I caught a buzz?"

"Fact that you ain't drunk is why I'm insisting that you tell me," Big Mo said.

"Thought I never made shit up?" Ray arched his eyebrows.

"Doesn't mean that what you got to say is gonna be more believable when your eyes are spinning round and your words are mush. Ray c'mon, talk to me," Big Mo forced a weak smile to her face.

Ray let out a loud sigh and motioned for the glass of whiskey. Big Mo hesitated. "C'mon, I'll talk. I promise." Ray held his hand out.

"Alright, but you lie to me and your next glass is gonna be filled with piss. Goes double for your friend there." Big Mo passed the glass to Ray.

"My name is Dubois," Dubois drained his glass and handed it back to Big Mo for a refill.

"Fine, Dubois," Big Mo passed the now full glass back. "Unless you like piss, make sure to fill in as many details as you can." Dubois nodded.

The music blaring inside The Dry Dock dropped low and Dubois could feel people pressing in around him and Ray. He guessed this was how gossip was always handled around this island, but doubted it had ever been like what he and Ray were about to report.

"Most of you heard what I had to say back there at the high school," Ray said. "I'm glad you had the good sense to leave that place and to come here where at least you'll be safe from the tidal surges."

"But what was all that bout a monster wrecking ships and what not?" a man asked. His words were neither sarcastic nor dismissive.

"Well, Cal," Ray answered. "That's the truth. I went out round the island and round Peach Island looking for your Bayliner and them beardoes that rented it. Course I didn't find them."

"Beardoes?" Dubois asked.

"That's Ray's word for weirdoes with beards," Cal answered. "He don't really like that kind too much." Cal paused and looked at some of the out of place looking patrons. "No offense meant of course, folks." The people smiled and waited for Ray to continue.

"We done with the vocab lesson for the day there, Cal?" Big Mo laughed. "My Lord, it's no wonder no one ever talks in here much – everyone would just cut 'em off. I remember that one time a few years ago when I was trying to tell ya bout –"

Ray cleared his throat and looked at Big Mo.

"Like I was saying," Big Mo grinned, "shut up and let Ray finish his damn story."

"Ain't no story," Ray looked into his glass of whiskey. The brown liquor offered no answers. "God knows I wish it were, but what I told you is real. There is something swimming around out there. I think it destroyed the Glaxco rig, sank Dubois' cargo ship and probably ate everyone one of them beardoes on Peach Island." Ray took a deep breath and drained his glass in one gulp. "We also saw it sink the ferry and everyone on it."

"You mean that Jimmy is –" Cal's words trailed off.

"He's dead," Ray nodded. "Me and Dubois were out there in my clam boat. We were going to stop Jimmy and get him to turn the ferry back towards Sunset, but we were too late." Ray stopped talking and stared down at the bar.

"The monster," Dubois continued the story, "had already climbed onto the ferry. We looked, but there was no one in the water. No emergency strobes. No cries for help. It came after us, but we outran it and made it back here."

"What do you mean when you say monster, cuz there's all sorts of monsters in this world, but I ain't yet to know of one that could wreck a rig and sink two large boats," Big Mo said. "I ain't saying that you're lying, but like most people, I don't know what the hell to make out of any of this."

"Fair enough," Dubois agreed. "I didn't think anything like this could exist either, but then something pinged on my ship's sonar. It was huge – a huge fucking thing. At first, I thought it was a tentacle, but after seeing the thing, I know it was its tail. It came out of the water and ripped my ship in two."

"Tentacle?" Cal asked. "Like a giant squid or octopus or something? You telling me that the damn Kraken is swimming round the waters off of Sunset?"

"More like Godzilla," Ray muttered. "It's some kind of reptile. I saw the damn thing walk right up outta the water and onto Peach Island."

"It came up onto land?" Big Mo gasped.

"Yeah," Ray answered. "Like I said, it was a giant fucking lizard. Thing can swim and walk around on land."

"And it chased after you when it was done with the ferry?" Cal chimed in.

"What's with the twenty questions?" Ray demanded. But the answers crept through is head. His brain had been packed in cotton from the night before and then everything went to shit out on the water. Ray was tired and now half-drunk and most definitely was not thinking straight.

Dubois had been attacked. A monster tried to eat him and succeeded in eating his whole crew. It was amazing that he wasn't curled up in the corner babbling like a loon and drawing pictures on the wall with his turds.

Neither of the men was thinking straight and had just been relieved to escape the nightmare they had faced, but had been too ragged to consider what might happen after they got to The Dry Dock.

"Turn off the lights!" Ray leapt up from his bar stool.

"Turn off the music!" Dubois commanded. "Big Mo, kill the generator!"

"Could've picked better word than kill, Dubois, don't you think?" Big Mo was already moving around the bar and out the back door.

"Everyone, move away from the windows and be as quiet as you can," Ray said. "If we stay quiet and just ride this out, we'll be okay. Once the storm blows out, someone will come to help us. All we need to do is sit tight and be quiet. Everything will be just fine, okay?"

Something *BOOMED* outside the bar, rattling the windows. They were already too late.

-24-

Ragged bits of ceiling tile fell like asbestos snowflakes around Mayor Billings. He could feel everything slipping through his sausage-like fingers. How was Sunset Island going to recover from this disaster? There had been other disasters – the ruptured sewer pipe that spilled raw sewage onto Sunset Beach, the one summer where the local morons thought it was hilarious to moon the ferry every time it came into port and even the time he had survived that disastrous recall vote. All of those crises had been managed, but this one threatened to end it all.

"We're leaving," Mayor Billings said to the crowd, but his voice had lost its force and conviction.

"What about the *tree* outside the school?" someone asked. "What are we going to do about that, huh?"

"Nothing," Mayor Billings snapped. "We're going out the back door of the auditorium. Whatever is outside, a tree or whatever, it is in the front of the school. It'll still be there. Let's go."

Mayor Billings brushed some dust from the falling ceiling and headed towards the back of the auditorium. He led everyone up onto the stage and behind the heavy red velvet curtains. A small door was set in the rear wall and led to the outside. Mayor Billings could hear the wind and rain through the door, but that was all. There was no crashing of downed trees or whatever else might be out there. It just sounded like a storm, albeit a bad one, but just a storm.

"Ready?" Mayor Billings made eye contact with each person he could see in the red glare of the emergency lights. No one said anything. He took that as agreement.

The wind whipped the rain around, throwing the droplets from every angle possible. The rain caught in the thick folds of Mayor Billings' neck, but he tried to ignore it and appear steadfast. These people were counting on him to lead. He was the mayor, damn it.

The street going north from the high school went up a small rise and disappeared behind a copse of trees.

"This way!" Mayor Billings shouted over his shoulder. He turned to make sure the people were still behind him, more for his security than out of a genuine sense of concern for the people following him.

The momentary turn was all Mayor Billings needed to catch a glimpse of the monster that slithered across the roof of the high school.

"It's not a tree," Mayor Billings round face jiggled as he stammered out the words.

"What are you talking about, Mayor?" some shouted over the wind.

The creature dropped from the second story roof, crushing a propane tank the size of a small car under its feet. The explosion threw a curling ball of fire high into the sky. If it affected the monster at all, it didn't let it show.

"It's a dragon! A dragon!" one of the children shrieked.

Seeing the monster in full detail, lit up by a wall of flames, Mayor Billings had to admit that it did indeed look like a dragon. His bacon soaked heart hammered in his chest, as if trying to break free of his slow body and run.

Mayor Billings ran towards the church, his thick legs carrying him as fast as they could. Citizens of Sunset Island and visitors screamed and ran. Some followed the mayor. Others took their chances away from the group.

Mayor Billings was sure people were shouting for him, demanding answers and leadership. The most the corpulent politician could manage as he wheezed up the hill was a repeated, "It's not a tree. It's not a tree."

-25-

The air inside of The Dry Dock was damp and oppressive. Groups of people were huddled throughout the dingy bar. Everyone seemed to be holding their breath, waiting for whatever had followed Ray and Dubois to show up.

Outside of the bar, the town of Sunset Island was silent. The only sounds were those of the hurricane, not that they brought comfort to anyone. The silence inside The Dry Dock was building and pressed down on everyone, becoming unbearable.

"That's it," Ray whispered. "I'm going outside to look." He turned and grabbed the bottle of whiskey from the top of the bar. Ray took a long pull from the bottle and walked towards the door, bottle still in hand. "Well, if that thing is gonna eat me, I might as well be drunk."

"Ray," Big Mo called in a hoarse whisper. The Captain turned and looked at the bartender, a smile on his sun burnt face. "Be careful, Ray, okay?"

Ray laughed. "Better cool it with all that mushy stuff, Big Mo. People might get to talking 'bout us."

"Mushy stuff?" Big Mo snorted. "You wish. I just don't want my best customer to get eaten by a fuckin' sea monster before he settles up on his tab. That's all I was saying, you big dummy." They both laughed.

The large brass ship's bell that hung on the door of The Dry Dock clanged loudly as Ray pushed the door open. He had heard that bell more times than he could remember and found comfort in it every time. But now the metallic clang sent icy bolts of fear lancing through his heart. Ray silently cursed himself for not holding the mallet still on the stupid bell. The damn thing had probably sounded like a dinner bell to that godless creature.

But the monster remained absent. Nothing slithered down the middle of the rain-choked street. Ray took a tentative step out of The Dry Dock. The wind gusted and he had to grab the door to steady himself.

Water gushed through the streets, chocking the gutters and pooling in the intersections. For now, it looked like The Dry Dock would be safe, but a strong storm surge could change all of that.

An Adirondack chair tumbled down the street past The Dry Dock. Bits of whitewashed wood trailed behind the chair as it made its way down the hill. Ray had a chair like that at home, not nearly as nice. That one had been one of those expensive magazine Adirondack chairs, not a homemade one cobbled together out of left over decking like Ray's. Still he would have given just about anything at that moment to be in his chair, a cold beer sweating in his fist and not a care in the world. Ray feared that the monster had swallowed up that life as well.

"How's it look?" Cal asked. He and Dubois stood in the doorway. The rain was changing Dubois' uniform back from khaki to black in a matter of seconds.

"Can you see where the explosion was?" Dubois asked.

In the distance, a faint ring of orange cut across the stormy night sky. The clouds fought to swallow the light and return Sunset to darkness.

"Over there," Ray pointed at the dying light. "Looks like it was at the high school. Probably one of the propane tanks, I'd guess."

"Maybe a tree fell on it and ruptured it? Cal offered optimistically.

"Yeah," Ray grunted. "And maybe I'm just too damn beautiful and that's why my wife left me."

"Well, you probably are better lookin' than the Big C," Cal sulked.

"That fuckin' lizard is probably better looking than the Big C," Ray said. "For God's sake, Cal, can we please focus on the fact that a sea monster is loose on our island? Please?"

"It's not exactly a sea monster," Cal shrugged.

"What the hell are you rambling on about, Cal?" Ray argued. Dubois was relieved to see Ray steering the conversation back to what mattered. "It came from the sea, so it's a sea monster. Plain and simple." Dubois had to stifle the urge to choke both men.

"I mean, it is on land now, so I'm just saying it might not be proper to call it a sea monster, is all," Cal replied.

"My God!" Dubois cried. "How the hell have you lived here for so long? Who cares what we call it? Call it François for all I care, but let's just get back to talking about it!"

"He's got a point," Cal nodded.

"Agreed," Ray shrugged. "So what do you think happened to everyone inside the high school?"

"Probably eaten by now," Dubois answered. "The monster made short work of my ship. I doubt a school building would be very difficult for it to destroy."

"Maybe the Mayor got them out?" Cal offered.

"The Mayor has a hard time getting outta his car," Ray snapped. "I wouldn't be counting on any heroics there."

"But all them people," Cal watched the flames flicker out.

"Nothing to be done," Ray shook his head sadly. "No point rushing off to save someone that might not be there."

The wind died down and Dubois cocked his head to the side. "Did you hear that? I could have sworn I heard a bell. There! There it was again!" The other men had heard the distant tone as well.

"A bell?" Cal looked around the empty street. "But that would have to be one huge freaking bell to be heard over all this mess."

"Like the one in the steeple of the church," Ray said. He listened to the tone again. There was a definite pattern to the ringing. "It's an SOS call. Someone's trying to call for help at the church."

"Good place to hole up," Cal agreed. "Nice and high with a strong foundation."

"None of that matters to the monster," Dubois scanned the street. "All it will hear is the dinner bell. We've got to go help them."

"Well, I guess I done more than my share of stupid for the day, so what's a little more gonna matter?" Ray said.

The bell was lost beneath a low roar. The sound rolled up the street towards the three men.

"What's that noise?" Dubois asked. "Thunder?"

"Ain't no thunder," Ray pointed to a wall of water moving up the street. "That's a damn tidal surge."

The water slammed into parked cars, throwing wide sprays of salty foam and swallowing the vehicles wholes. The surge of storm waters obscured the men's view of the rest of Sunset Island. It didn't look like it would get to the top of the hill, but it sure as hell was going to make rescuing the people in the church a lot harder.

"Am I going crazy or are those..." Cal pointed at the waves.

"Fins," Ray finished his friend's sentence. "Ain't that a bitch?"

Things had just gone from bad to worse.

-26-

Mayor Billings counted seven people inside the church. I was dark, but between flashes of lightning, he had double-checked his count. Only seven remained. There had been close to twenty or thirty when he left the high school. Now there were only seven, two crying children and five adults in various states of shock.

Some people had tried to run in different directions, instead of heading to the church. Maybe they had survived. Mayor Billings doubted it, though. That creature, that fucking nightmare from the age of dinosaurs had been relentless in its pursuit. There was no way those people had survived.

Images of running towards the church played through Mayor Billings' head like a 1950's creature feature movie. The giant lizard stormed off the roof of the high school, exploding a propane tank beneath its scaly feet and came after them. It emerged from the shadows engulfing the street and plucked mouthfuls of people from the line behind Mayor Billings. The Mayor momentarily stopped, maybe out of concern but more likely out of fatigue and second helpings, to see the monster attack. It plowed through the trees lining the sides of Poplar Street, ripping them up by the roots and tossing them aside. People froze in panic and the monster feasted.

Organs and meat, all raw and red, rained down from the creature's mouth, slapping loudly when it hit the wet pavement and slithered down the street, carried by small streams of rainwater. Mayor Billings kept running. Screams and weak cries let him know the monster wasn't far behind.

The church loomed at the top of the hill like a white, steepled beacon of hope and safety. Mayor Billings pushed the heavy doors closed, not caring that people were still outside, still food for the monster. Seven slipped through the doors before Mayor Billings dropped the heavy bar, locking the thick oak doors. These doors were strong, at least six inches of solid oak, and banded with thick brass fittings. They were safe. Mayor Billings had saved them, all seven of them.

"Well, what do we do now?" a man asked. He wore a linen suit that had become soaked and left nothing to the imagination. His tightie-whities peeked through the transparent pants like the sad uniform of a super hero. The man appeared to be beyond caring.

"Do?" Mayor Billings panted. That bit of running had been more exercise than he had done in the last ten years. He was in no rush to do anything, aside from catching his breath. "We're not going to do anything. I got us here and we're safe. There's nothing left to do, other than wait for help."

"Wait for help?" Tighty Whities snapped. "How is anyone even going to know we're here, let alone that we need help?"

"I'm open to suggestions," Mayor Billings shrugged. He took out his cell phone and checked the signal. It was dead. "There's no signal on my cell phone. I'm guessing the hurricane knocked down the service tower. Land lines are probably gone too."

"What about a radio or something?" Tighty Whities demanded. "I would have thought that every townie on this fucking island had a CB and police scanner in their house. Isn't that what you people do for entertainment around here?" A few others echoed the sentiment.

"It may surprise you to learn that we received the magical box that fancy folks like yourself call television about a century ago. We've also raised our literacy rate significantly." Mayor Billings smiled, though the expression held no humor. "But yes, regardless of how much of an asshole my friend here is, he does have a point. Many houses do have those things, but none of that matters right now."

"Why not?" Tighty Whities asked.

"Because we're not in a fucking house!" Mayor Billings' voice boomed and echoed in the empty church. "Since we're busy wasting time talking about shit that doesn't matter and won't help us, why not discuss the merits of a tank or naval strike?" Mayor Billings appeared to fall deep into thought. "Wait a second, that might be it!"

"You have a tank?" Tighty Whities asked hopefully.

"You sure are dumb, mister," a small boy sniffled.

"From the mouths of babes," Mayor Billings tried to muss the boy's sandy hair, but he ducked the Mayor's hammy hand and slid into an empty pew. "Well, anyway. No, the comment I made about a naval strike made me think. Perhaps we need to employ a means of communication a bit more primitive than our cell phones and radios."

"Like what?" Tighty Whities looked around the church for an answer.

"Like the bell in the church's tower." Mayor Billings pointed to the ceiling of the church. "We can use the bell to send an SOS and I'm sure there have to be some lanterns or flashlights in the basement. It's our best bet, our only one really."

"Ring the bell?" Tighty Whities laughed. "That's your ingenious master plan? Isn't that going to let the monster know that we're in here? Why not just open the front doors and invite it in?"

"You fucking moron. It chased us here, remember?" Mayor Billings seethed. "Don't you think it already knows that we're in here? What more harm can be done by ringing the bell and flashing a light?"

"Fine," Tighty Whities collapsed into a pew. "It's your plan, so you do it."

"That was my plan all along," Mayor Billings chuckled. "Do you honestly think I'd trust you to do it? You'd spend all your time trying to figure out how to spell 'S-O-S' and then probably do it wrong anyway. Just sit here and shut up. Think you can handle that?"

Everyone remained silent. Mayor Billings nodded and walked to the back of the church. After a few minutes of searching, he emerged with a large flashlight.

"Alright, does anyone know the Morse code for SOS?" Mayor Billings asked. "Anyone? Come on now, it's just a bunch of dots and dashes. Anyone?"

"I know it," the sandy haired boy raised his hand. "I was a scout."

"Wonderful," Mayor Billings nodded. "So you will climb into the tower and signal with the light while I ring the bell."

"Hold up now," Tighty Whities said. "Why not the reverse? Let the kid ring the bell and you go up in the tower."

"I'm afraid that will not be an option," Mayor Billings shook his head.

"Why not?" Tighty Whites demanded.

"Because the opening is too narrow," Mayor Billings said in an almost whisper.

"Great!" Tighty Whities slapped the pew with his palm. "Because you're too fucking fat, a kid has to go up there and do it."

"Would you like to take his place?" Mayor Billings smiled.

"The kid is a scout," Tighty Whities protested. "Said so himself. Seems like a scout is the best choice to signal."

"Just give me the flashlight already." The kid held his hand out. Mayor Billings handed it to him. He slipped the flashlight into his belt and tore two pages out of a hymnal. Crumpling up the paper, the boy stuffed bits of it into his ears. "Okay. Where's the ladder? I'm ready."

The boy scrambled up the narrow ladder that was little more than rough lengths of timber hastily nailed together. It creaked under his slight weight, but he continued upwards. As he climbed higher, the boy couldn't help but wonder why no one bothered to ask his name. It was Daniel, not that they seemed to care. His parents had cared, had named him after his mom's dad, but they were gone. The monster had seen to that. Maybe the people down in the church didn't want to know his name. Maybe it was easier to send him to his death as an anonymous shadowy face, not as Daniel, the kid whose parents were just eaten.

A trap door loomed above Daniel's head. He wrapped an arm around the top rung of the ladder and fumbled with the lock with his free hand. A faint *click* signaled his success and he pushed the door open.

Wind whipped through the round slatted windows of the bell tower, blowing a cold misty rain through the narrow openings. Daniel figured no one would care if he knocked away a few slats so the light would be more visible. Honestly,

Daniel knew it probably didn't matter if the shone the SOS signals straight up his ass. No one was going to see it through the storm and anyone who did wasn't going to be able to help. But doing something seemed better than doing nothing.

Pulling the heavy flashlight from his belt, Daniel battered at the slatted windows until a few sections broke and fell away. He peered through the opening. It didn't look like the monster was out there or at least it wasn't right in front of the church.

Daniel jumped and almost dropped the flashlight out the window as the bell clanged behind him. That fat fucking mayor was eager to pull the rope. The bell's vibrations danced through Daniel's skin and jangled his bones. He was glad to have stuffed his ears, but the sound was still overwhelming.

The light shone out and Daniel used his hand to cut off the beam in the correct sequence for SOS. Then he moved to another window, broke the slats and signaled again. Something roared outside the church, but it wasn't the monster. Daniel had heard it eat his parents and it barely made a sound.

Running to the other side of the tower, Daniel broke away the slats and tried to see where the noise was coming from. A wall of frothy seawater rolled up the street towards the church. Daniel turned to warn everyone inside the church, but as he pulled out one of his earplugs, he could already hear them screaming. The church was flooding.

Danny ran back to the window to see how deep both the water and trouble was for everyone inside the church. It had already crept up the stairs and was beginning to slip under the door. More kept coming.

Something dark cut back and forth through the turbulent storm waters. It was soon joined by another shape. Then another. And another. The water looked alive, like a thin skin stretched across the muscled back of some terrible beast.

Twisting the head of the flashlight, Daniel focused the beam and shone it down on the water. The gray, torpedo-like head of a shark shone just beneath the surface. The shark's fins and tails thrashed, cutting the water and throwing arcs of foam. One moved up the stairs. It bumped its nose on the second to last step and turned to swim away.

Soon the water would reach the top and so would the sharks.

-27-

"See," Ray pointed, "Told you not to bother with tying up my clam boat. Ain't you glad that you listened?" Dubois watched as Ray's boat bobbed in the storm surge that inched towards The Dry Dock.

"We can worry about that later," Dubois said. "Let's get back inside and figure out what we're going to do."

All eyes inside The Dry Dock turned to look at the three rain soaked men that stood in the doorway. They wanted answers, but there were none to give.

"Storm surge is rolling in," Ray began. "Looks like it already flooded the lower parts of town and it's making its way here. I'd say we got maybe thirty minutes, an hour at the most before the water is coming through the front door."

"Well, we can deal with that," Big Mo said. "Lil' bit of water ain't nothing to worry about compared to a god damn sea monster."

"We were talking about that," Cal began. "You see, the monster…"

"Shut up, Cal!" Dubois and Ray shouted in unison. Cal looked offended, but stayed quiet.

"The water ain't the worst of it," Ray continued. "And we didn't see any sign of the monster. I think it's over by the church. God help them folks. They were ringing the bell as an SOS."

"So if it ain't the monster or the water, then what's got all three of your short hairs all tied up in a knot?" Big Mo asked. She cast a quick glance out the window. Small waves spat foam against the bar's windows as they crashed into the curb in front of the bar.

"It's the sharks," Dubois answered.

"Sharks?" Big Mo questioned.

"Yes," Dubois nodded. "We could see a handful of fins gliding through the water. They'll be here as soon as the water is high enough."

A sudden surge of seawater rushed past The Dry Dock. The large glass windows in front of the bar began to look like oversized fish tanks. First, it was only smaller fish, but soon the large shadowy shape of a shark glided past the windows. The water kept climbing higher.

"The water is coming in faster," Dubois backed away from the windows. Small cracks spread across the glass like the work of thousands of invisible spiders.

"Them windows ain't gonna hold," Big Mo shouted. "Everyone move to the kitchen. There's a ladder by the sink that leads up to the roof. Get your asses up there."

People inside The Dry Dock began to panic.

"Go!" Ray yelled. "Stop screwing around and get up to that roof." Dubois and Cal began pushing people into the kitchen. Cal scrambled up the ladder and pushed open the heavy metal trapdoor. A gust of wind and rain rushed down through the opening, soaking the people below.

A loud crash sounded from the front of the bar. Cal pulled the last of the people onto the roof as Ray spilled out onto the slick roof. Puddles grew in the divots on the roof, making the tarpaper glisten.

"Where's Big Mo?" Cal shouted over the wind.

"What'd you mean?" Ray called back. "Isn't she up here?"

"I didn't see her come up the ladder," Cal answered.

"She must be trapped in the bar," Dubois moved back to the trapdoor. Seawater was already filling the kitchen below.

"I got it," Ray moved Dubois aside. "You and Cal get the clam boat so we can get the hell off this roof and over to the church."

"Be careful," Cal yelled over the wind.

"Ain't I always?" Ray grinned before he slid down the ladder.

-28-

"Hey, kid, are you coming down from there?" Mayor Billings shouted into the bell tower.

"My name is Daniel and no, I'm not coming down," Daniel called back. He could see the outline of the mayor at the bottom of the ladder. The sloshing of water could also be heard.

"Come on down, Daniel," Mayor Billings said with feigned cheeriness. "Don't worry about a little bit of water. Just come on down."

"You just want me to come down so the rest of you can climb up here," Daniel shouted back. They had sent him into the bell tower because it was dangerous and none of them was brave enough to do it. Now they wanted to trade places. Daniel looked around the bell tower. There was enough space for some people, not many and certainly not that fat ass, Mayor Billings.

"No, no," Mayor Billings said. He looked down. The water was already at his knees. "Look, Danny. I can call you Danny, right?"

"My mom did," Daniel said.

"Okay, great then, Danny," Mayor Billings continued.

"My mom is dead," Daniel shouted back. "She's dead because you're a dumb ass and led everyone outside, so don't you dare call me Danny."

"Alright, fine," Mayor Billings said. "Daniel, look it's safer for you down here."

"You mean it's safer for you up here," Daniel said. "Besides, I'm stuck. I can't come down."

"What do you mean you're stuck?" Mayor Billings asked.

"Some floorboards broke and my ankle is trapped," Daniel lied. He wasn't going back down there, but there were other kids that he couldn't leave down there either. "Send up the other kids to help me pull my leg free. There isn't enough room for adults. Send them up to get me free and then I'll come down."

"Fine, fine," Mayor Billings groaned and turned to the remaining children. "You heard him. Go up there and get him loose. Make sure you come right back down. No funny business. Got it?" The three children nodded.

Daniel moved away from the trapdoor as the three children climbed into the bell tower.

"Any of you have parents down there?" Daniel asked.

The children all shook their heads. "No, the monster got them too, just like your parents."

"So none of you feel bad about staying up here?" Daniel asked.

Again, the children shook their heads.

"Good, because I saw sharks in the water and it won't be long before they get inside. I think we're better off up here," Daniel said. "My name is Daniel, by the way."

"I'm Cameron. Most people call me Cam. These are my little sisters, Abby and Annie. They're twins and kind of freaky, but don't let it get to you," Cameron said.

"Cam, twins are the least of freaky that's going around today," Daniel smirked. "Close the trapdoor."

Below Mayor Billings heard the echo of the trapdoor slamming shut and the heavy bolt sliding into place. Moments later, the front doors of the church burst open.

-29-

The water was coming in fast. Ray had seen his share of storms and flooding had been part of some of them, but not like this. Islands like Sunset always had a strong vein of superstition with undercurrents of folklore. The old timers mumbled about storms that only happened once every few hundred years. Some even got drunk enough to slur stories about the mythical monsters that the storms woke, but Ray had never taken any of their talk as anything more than the creation of small town boredom. Recently, he was beginning to think they had been onto something.

The swinging door leading out of the kitchen felt heavy. Ray planted his shoulder in the middle of the door and pushed forward. Cold seawater rushed through the opening with a salty spray.

"Ray, get your dumb ass up off the floor," Big Mo shouted from where she stood on the top of the bar.

"C'mon," Ray waved his hand towards the door. Why was Big Mo waiting? The water was high, but certainly not high enough to keep her from getting to the kitchen. "What the hell is keeping you?"

A gray fin rose out of the water near the pool table. It cut through the dark water throwing small waves to the sides that splashed across the green velvet. The fin circled the pool table before heading towards Ray.

"You gonna get off the floor now, you big dummy?" Big Mo shouted as she hurled a glass beer pitcher at the shark. She missed, but the animal turned away and swam back towards the pool table.

Ray sloshed through the water and climbed onto the top of the bar next to Big Mo. "Okay, so there's a shark in here, but it's over by the pool table and the kitchen is right over there," Ray pointed. "It's scary, but it ain't much more than eight feet or so, Big Mo. A shark that size probably won't take much interest in you and me. That thing probably got pushed in by the storm and is busy looking for fish. Now, c'mon, let's get the hell outta here before real trouble shows up."

"You're lucky you're cute, Ray, cuz you sure as hell ain't smart." Big Mo watched the shark swim past the bar. The water was still rising and soon it would be level with the top of the bar.

"What the hell are you talking about?" Ray asked. The shark did another loop around the pool table before heading back towards the bar. Its tail thrashed in the water as it increased its pace. Ray watched the shark's head crest above the foamy water as its sleek body gained speed.

The shark launched itself out of the water towards the bar. A spray of water and blood splashed across Ray's face. His trembling hands wiped the gore away from his eyes. He was almost too scared to look to his side and see what was left of Big Mo.

"You okay?" Ray's voice shook as he asked the question. "You, uh, alright over there, Big Mo?" Ray forced his eyes open.

Big Mo was still standing on the bar. She spat as blood streaked down her face and into her mouth. The lower half of a shark bobbed in the water, as thick tendrils of blood twisted away like black ribbons. A second shark, at least two times the size of the other, swam towards the back of The Dry Dock. Ray could see the other half of the first shark between its jaws.

"*That* is what was keeping me, you big dummy," Big Mo pointed.

-30-

"Come on, kids, just open up the door," Tighty Whities tapped on the trapdoor. The ladder creaked under his weight as he shifted to knock again with a little more force this time. "Daniel, you need to open this door right now."

"I can't do that," Daniel said. "Sorry mister, but the floor is too rotten up here. It wouldn't hold your weight and sure as all heck wouldn't hold the mayor."

"Kid, I don't give a shit about the mayor or anyone else down here," Tighty Whities continued. "Just let me up there and then we can lock the door again. Come on, Daniel, I can help you."

"Like when you helped me before?" Daniel asked.

"What are you talking about kid?" Tighty Whities said.

"When we left the high school," Daniel answered. "Everyone down there ran right past our parents as the monster ate them. None of you even stopped to see if we needed help."

"I didn't see you out there. I didn't see anyone," Tighty Whities said.

"Of course you didn't," Daniel snorted. "Because you were too busy looking out for yourself. So like I said before, sorry, but this door is staying shut."

"Open the fucking door, you little shit," Tighty Whities shouted. He smashed his fist against the trapdoor. "Open it! Open it right now!" He stomped his foot on the rung of the ladder.

"Oh, well since you asked so nicely," Daniel paused, "then no."

Cam looked at Daniel. Doubt was clearly etched into his young face. Annie and Abby huddled in the corner. "Daniel, you really think the floor would break if we let some of them up here?"

"Some? No," Daniel answered. "I think the floor is fine. But it's not some of them that I'm worried about. It's all of them. Besides, they didn't give a crap about us, so they'll just have to figure it out for themselves. I'm sorry, Cam, but there's no way I'm opening that door."

"He's right, Cam," one of the twins said. Daniel thought it might be Abby, but couldn't be sure. "We're safe right now. If we open the door, we won't be safe anymore. Please listen to Daniel."

"Okay," Cam sighed. "But I really don't think we're safe."

"I know," Daniel nodded. "We're not. Sharks and water is one thing, but there's still a monster out there."

"Do you think maybe it left, like it swam away or something?" Cam asked. "We haven't seen it for awhile now. Maybe it's gone?"

"Gone?" Daniel said. "No, I don't think it's gone."

"Why not?" Cam asked.

"I remember when I was working on Environmental Science and Oceanography badges in Scouts," Daniel answered. "I studied a lot of different animals, but one thing was pretty much always the same."

"What's that?" one of the twins asked.

Daniel took in a deep breath and let it out slowly. "Animals never go too far from their food source."

-31-

Ray's clam boat bobbed on the other side of the street. The storm surge had pushed it towards The Dry Dock, but being on the other side of the street still felt like a world away.

"So how are we going to get Ray's boat?" Dubois asked.

"Damned if I know," Cal said. "But we better figure it out quick."

"Maybe the storm will carry it over here," Dubois offered, though he knew it was a long shot.

"Yeah, and maybe those sharks down there have suddenly gone vegetarian," Cal said. "And maybe that monster up and left too since we're busy talking about shit that ain't gonna happen."

Dubois looked around the roof. Cal was right. The sharks and water were a problem, but the monster was still somewhere on the island. It had gone after the *Ponce De Leon* with a single-minded focus, so there was no way it was going to leave this much food behind. At best, the monster was full after eating everyone on the *Ponce De Leon*, Peach Island and at the high school, but that wouldn't last forever. The sharks and water were a distraction. They needed to focus on getting the boat, getting the people in the church and getting the hell off of Sunset Island before the monster got hungry again. There weren't many people. Dubois figured he could probably fit all of them in Ray's boat, but first he had to get it.

"Okay, so I guess that only leaves us one option then?" Dubois stared at the clam boat on the other side of the street.

"You're thinking about swimming over there, aren't you?" Cal asked.

"Unless you've got a better idea," Dubois said.

"Better?" Cal replied. "No, I can't think of a better one."

"Then what are we talking about?" Dubois demanded.

"Which one of us is gonna do it," Cal answered.

"I'll do it," Dubois said. "There. Debate over, now let's get the boat."

"Dubois, you've already had seven shades of shit beat out of you today," Cal said. "Don't you think it's a better idea to let me do it?"

"Probably," Dubois nodded. He stepped on the ledge of The Dry Dock's roof and leapt into the water below. Cal was right. Dubois was tired, but he was also at least a decade younger than Cal and figured he had the best chance of getting to the boat. It still didn't make the decision any more enjoyable.

Dubois had spent most of his life on ships and near the ocean. He had swum beside just about every animal in the sea, including sharks. Most of the time, sharks had no interest in people. Most of the time, sharks only bit someone because they mistook them for a seal or something like that. This wasn't most of the time.

The splash Dubois made when he hit the water startled the sharks and scattered them around the street. Dubois remained still and let the sharks calm down before he started swimming. The water was chest deep. Dubois walked to the edge of the sidewalk and stood still, his toes dangling off the curb. A shark circled around his legs, investigating the source of the splash before swimming back towards The Dry Dock.

Dubois took a deep breath and let his body weight carry him off the curb and into the street. The water was cold, but Dubois hardly noticed. All he could see was Ray's boat. It was all he could focus on. Not the sharks, not the monster, only the boat. It was the only thing that existed.

Cal watched Dubois begin swimming towards Ray's boat. A good number of the sharks had moved down the street with the water. Some had gone inside The Dry Dock and a few still circled in the water out front. The sharks were large and Cal had no idea what kind they were, but figured he could wonder about details like that after he got everyone safely into the boat.

Dubois had made it most of the way across the street and was about the grab the side of Ray's boat when a rush of water moved it further down the street. Dubois disappeared under the water. Maybe he had hit his head. Was he knocked out?

"Shit," Cal growled as he moved closer to the edge of the bar's roof. Dubois remerged from under the water and waved that he was fine. He spat a mouthful of salt water before continuing after the boat. Cal felt a moment of relief. Dubois was okay. They could still get the boat and get the hell out of here.

Cal watched three black fins rise out of the water behind Dubois. The other man had no idea that the sharks were behind him. If the sharks got Dubois, they would have no hope of getting to the boat. Blood in the water would make every other shark in the area crazy. There would be a feeding frenzy and the water would just keep climbing higher.

"Everyone, be ready as soon as Dubois gets back with that boat," Cal said to the people on the roof. Through the wind and rain, it was hard to tell if they heard or answered him, but they would know what to do. Cal knew what he needed to do.

Stepping onto the edge of the roof, Cal looked down at the dark water below. He couldn't see any sharks, but they were down there. Cal stepped off the ledge.

A wide spray of foamy water shot sideways as Cal hit the water. He remembered hearing on a nature show that sharks responded to vibrations or electrical signals in the water or something like that. He hoped they responded to cursing and slapping the water too.

"Come on, you nasty bastards," Cal shouted as he slammed his open palms down on the surface of the water. "Come back this way, you salty fucks."

Two of the fins behind Dubois turned back towards The Dry Dock. The third stayed behind him. The lyrics to a Meatloaf song began running through Cal's head as he continued to yell and slap the water. He wished that his final moment had a better soundtrack, but guessed it could be worse. The two sharks picked up speed. Their fins cut through the water like knives as the closed the distance between them and Cal.

Two out of three ain't bad, but Cal doubted that The Almighty Loaf had sharks in mind when he was singing that song. Hell, one was bad enough, let alone two, but Cal had to buy Dubois enough time to reach Ray's boat. Two? Three? Whatever. Cal figured it would have to be enough.

-32-

Mayor Billings watched the first shark come through the doors of the church. He watched it grab a woman around the waist and thrash violently as bits of meat and intestine were thrown like confetti. He watched the woman cry out in agony as a second shark tore her leg free. Red, foamy water spilled down the aisle of the church and washed against the white marble steps leading up to the altar.

Leadership? Answers? Screw it. Mayor Billings had done his job, had shouldered his burden and got everyone, well not everyone, this far. He was done trying to save people who weren't willing to save themselves. Mayor Billings threw open a door on the side of the altar that lead into the sacristy. People were screaming inside of the church. Mayor Billings locked the door behind him.

Frantic fists beat against the door. Screams demanded that Mayor Billings open it. He ignored both. His job was done. Sunset Island was done. It was time to begin worrying about numero uno. A gush of red water spilled under the door and splashed against Mayor Billings' boots, which were, oddly enough, sharkskin. There was divine irony somewhere in that situation, but Mayor Billings didn't have time to enjoy it.

A second door led out of the sacristy and into a narrow hallway. Mayor Billings wheezed and puffed. Water was already spilling into the hallway. Red water.

The rear doors of the church had water slipping between the doors and the jamb. It was fortunately not red. Mayor Billings' heart thumped in his chest like a coked out rabbit. At any moment, he was sure it would burst through his ribcage and splatter against the heavy wooden doors leading outside.

The screams inside the church had gone silent. Mayor Billings could hear the wind whipping against the trees outside, but the silence inside of the church was oppressive. Images of a tomb flashed through Mayor Billings' head. It was time to go. The heavy oak doors resisted as Mayor Billings pushed from one side and water from the other. Once the space looked large enough, Mayor Billings wedged his round frame between the two doors and tried to wriggle out. His stomach and belt buckle caught on the opposing door.

"Damn it," Mayor Billings seethed and tried to suck in his considerable gut.

Ripples undulated across the waist deep water. Mayor Billings looked around. Maybe another person had escaped from inside of the church. He would be glad to have company, or at least someone to help him get his belly free.

A loud splashed sounded somewhere near the old cemetery behind the church. Was it a shark? Flames danced across distant trees that had been struck by lightning.

The trees swayed in the wind, some more than others. Four, in fact, appeared to be moving towards the church. A giant lizard slithered out of the cemetery's shadows. Lightning flashed, throwing the monster's greenish black visage into stark contrast against the dark sky. Hard, scaly angles jutted from the monster's massive head. Horns spiked from its brow and lips. Its yellow eyes caught the reflection from the distant fires and glowed with a cold, single-minded hunger.

Mayor Billings thrashed and tried to pull himself free, but as the creature moved closer, it pushed more water against the doors. Mayor Billings was stuck. He tried to remain calm. Tried not to piss his pants. He failed on both fronts.

The monster dropped down and slithered through the water in a wide curving motion. It stopped and eyed Mayor Billings. Its forked tongue flicked the air, tasting it. The monster's rough lips curled back revealing a tangled nest of wicked needle-like teeth set into tar black gums. With a quick snap of its head, the creature closed its jaws around the upper half of Mayor Billings and wrenched him free with a hard tug.

Mayor Billings watched wide-eyed as he left his lower half wedged between the rear doors of the church. A thick coil of intestine spun downwards, trailing like a hellish party streamer. The mayor's hands pawed at the slick meaty rope, pulling it towards him as if in an attempt to reel in his lower half and put both sides back together.

The creature flicked Mayor Billings upper half into the air. He disappeared in a gnashing of teeth and crunching of bone. The heavy rope of intestine splashed into the water below where an army of smaller sharks fought over the remains of the mayor.

It was dark inside The Dry Dock. Ray could see shadows and knew what they were from memory. In truth, if he had been blindfolded Ray would have an easier time finding his way through The Dry Dock than his own house. There was the pool table, jukebox, and the broken cigarette machine that Big Mo refused to throw out. All the shadows and shapes were where they were supposed to be. Everything was where it was supposed to be. Except for one thing, one big thing.

The shark cut back and forth from one side of The Dry Dock to the other. It had yet to attempt a jump like the smaller shark had, but Ray figured it was only a matter of time. The shark turned, its tail knocking aside a few tables that floated in the water. It thrashed and swam into the kitchen through the open door.

"Well, what the hell do we do now?" Ray groaned. "That damn thing is in the kitchen."

Big Mo looked around The Dry Dock. She was probably the only person on Sunset Island that knew the bar better than Ray. She knew every inch of the bar, had hung each bit of nautical memorabilia on the wall, including the harpoon. Big Mo grabbed the harpoon and yanked it off the wall. The screws resisted, but the bartender was able to wrench it free from where it hung. The shaft of the harpoon was splintered in a few spots and the spearhead was rusted, but it was still a harpoon.

"Let's go." Big Mo edged around Ray and continued down the bar. The water was already washing over the top of the bar, but Big Mo walked confidently towards the kitchen.

"Big Mo," Ray said, "hold up a second now. You can't just storm into the kitchen with that old harpoon in your hands."

"The hell I can't," Big Mo snapped. "This bar might be full of water and have Jaws in the kitchen, but it's still my damn bar and no fish is going to change that." Big Mo grabbed the top of the doorjamb and looked into the kitchen. "It's over by the sink. Hold the harpoon and I'm gonna jump to the nearest counter." She held out the harpoon.

Ray took the spear and turned it over in his hands. "You sure about this, Big Mo? This thing looks older than the two of us combined."

"Is the end still pointy and sharp?" Big Mo asked.

Ray touched the end of the harpoon with his index finger. "Yeah, I guess so."

"Then shut your mouth and get your ass in gear." Big Mo smiled before she swung into the kitchen. Her boots swept through the water. Ray heard a splash as Big Mo landed on the top of the counter. She leaned through the door and motioned for the harpoon.

"You ready?" Ray held out the harpoon.

"Ready as I'll ever be," Big Mo took the weapon.

"So what's the plan?" Ray asked.

"Plan?" Big Mo snorted. "I'm gonna stick the pointy end of this harpoon into the shark's head and then we're gonna get the hell outta here."

"Okay, sure," Ray nodded. "But how are we gonna get the shark to come back over here?"

"Well, that's the part you ain't gonna like much," Big Mo replied. "You're gonna have to draw the shark out."

"Draw it out?" Ray asked. "You mean you want me to get in the water and bait the damn thing?"

"Don't get soft on me now, Ray," Big Mo said. "I still got the shit end of this deal cuz once it's over here, I gotta jump on its back and stab the damn thing."

Ray opened his mouth to argue or offer a different plan, but there wasn't one. This was it. Ray slipped off the bar and stood in the kitchen doorway. The water was almost to his armpits.

"Go on and slap the water or something," Big Mo motioned. Ray nodded and began slapping the water.

The kitchen was dark and Ray couldn't see where the shark was, but could hear the water sloshing. Somewhere deep inside the kitchen a pot banged with a hollow *clunk*. The shark was coming.

The water rose up in a small wall. Ray could see the tail of the shark thrashing above the water as it powered towards him.

"Big Mo?" Ray asked as he continued to slap the water.

"Move," Big Mo screamed as she launched herself off of the countertop.

Ray tried to move quickly, but the water slowed his progress. The best he could manage was to press his back against the bar and try to stay out of the way.

The shark turned towards Ray. He was pretty sure he was going to die. Maybe death by shark would somehow be less awful than death by sea monster. Ray figured either was going to suck.

Big Mo let a loud string of creatively strung curse words fly as she crashed onto the back of the shark. She drove the point of the harpoon into the soft flesh on top of its head. Blood welled from the wound. The shark thrashed wildly, throwing Big Mo off its back. She held half of the harpoon's shaft in her hand. The other half had been driven into the shark. The shark, which swam out into the bar, did a turn and headed back for Ray and Big Mo.

"It's coming back," Ray said.

"Ideas?" Big Mo asked.

"Toss me the stick! Toss me the stick," Ray shouted. He held his hands out. Big Mo threw him the remaining section of the harpoon. "Stay still."

Big Mo stood in the doorway waiting for the shark. She could see the broken section of harpoon cutting through the water. She hoped Ray knew what he was doing.

The shark's head lifted out of the water. It opened its mouth to reveal pink gums that jutted forward with row upon row of ivory daggers set in them.

Ray grabbed the broken section of harpoon sunken into the shark's head and twisted it towards him. The shark, caught off guard, flipped sideways. It thrashed and tried to right itself. Ray plunged the other section of harpoon shaft into the shark's cold black eye. The shark thrashed a few more times; each spasm weaker than the last until it finally went still.

"Let's go," Big Mo waved towards the ladder. Water began rushing into The Dry Dock through the smashed windows. No one wanted to wait around to see what came through the window with the water.

"Just sucks," Ray muttered as he climbed the ladder behind Big Mo.

"What sucks?" Big Mo demanded. "Don't tell me you're feeling bad for that shark down there."

"No, it ain't that," Ray said as he climbed out and stood on the roof.

"Well, then what is it?" Big Mo asked.

"I just landed the biggest fish of my life and ain't nobody gonna believe me," Ray laughed.

Big Mo laughed too, but stopped when she saw the other people on the roof or more importantly the people that weren't on the roof. "Where the hell are Dubois and Cal?"

No one answered, but a few fingers pointed towards the edge of the roof.

-34-

It was difficult to listen to all the people in the church screaming. The water and high ceilings made for strange and horrific echoes. Once they went silent, Daniel unlatched the trapdoor and peered into the darkness below.

"Pass me the flashlight," he held out his hand. Cam flicked the light on and gave it Daniel. The narrow beam of yellow light didn't show much, but what it did capture was terrible. A frothy red sea waited at the bottom of the ladder. Unidentifiable chunks of raw meat bobbed in stew. Daniel panned the light to the side and gagged as he caught a chewed length of leg with a partial foot in the beam. Ribbons of tattered muscle and skin waved like crimson ribbons where the body parts were close to the surface.

Daniel clicked the light off and sat back against the wall of the bell tower.

"It's really bad down there," Daniel said softly. Tears streaked down his face and splattered on the rough planks that made up the floor. He didn't want the people inside the church to die, but he didn't want to die himself. They would have thrown him and the other kids out of the tower and that could be Daniel's leg bobbing in the water below. He had made a difficult choice, a terrible one, but it was the right one. Still, it didn't make the images below any easier to accept.

Cam lay on his stomach and panned the flashlight back and forth. A few fins could still be seen moving through the crimson water, picking on the ragged bits of meat that floated on the surface. After a few minutes, he sat back and took a deep breath. "It's not your fault, Daniel," Cam said. "The sharks did that, not you. They would have left us down there. You didn't have a choice."

"I guess not," Daniel muttered from where he had buried his face in his folded arms. "But what do we do now?"

"I don't know," Cam admitted. "The sharks are still down there, so I don't think we can go that way. And it looks like the water is still rising, but I doubt it could get this high, right?"

"No, I don't think it will," Daniel stood up and wiped his nose with the back of his hand. There would be time to be sad later. Right now, he had to figure out what they were going to do. "We could try ringing the bell again or signaling with the flashlight."

"Do you think anyone heard it last time?" Cam asked.

"Cam?" one of the twins asked.

"Not right now, Annie," Cam turned, "I mean, Abby. We're busy."

"But Cam," Abby persisted. She pointed outside.

"What Abby? What is it?" Cam groaned. Little sisters could be so annoying sometimes and twins were twice as bad. He didn't have time for her little kid games.

"Something heard the bell," Abby pointed.

"What do you mean something?" Daniel asked.

"Yeah, don't you mean someone, not something?" Cam demanded.

"Nope," Abby answered. "Something heard the bell."

Cam and Daniel rushed over to where Abby peered out between the slats of the bell tower window. Below, a giant shape moved with feline grace around the side of the church.

"Holy shit," Cam gasped. "You were right, Daniel. It's back. It's down there. It looks like a dragon. How is that possible? How is there a dragon out there? What do we do?"

Daniel wanted to panic. He wanted to scream. He wanted to cry. "Just be quiet and stay still," Daniel forced out between his chattering teeth. "Don't make any noise." Cam was right – there was a dragon outside the church and Daniel had no idea what to do.

Annie shifted her feet as she climbed to the window next to Abby and the boys. Large motes of dust spiraled upwards from the floor. Annie's face wrinkled.

"No, Annie. Don't. Please don't," Cam tried to stop his little sister but it was too late.

A thunderous sneeze exploded from her petite nose and echoed off the inside of the large metal bell that hung in the middle of the tower.

The dragon's head snapped in the direction of the tower. Its massive forked tongue danced in the air.

"Maybe it didn't hear us," Annie said.

The snap and crunch of wood filled the tower as it shook and tilted. Daniel took one more look through the slated window to see the monstrous lizard clawing its way towards the top.

"It heard," Daniel choked.

"What do we do?" Cam asked. His words were raw and strained. "We're stuck Daniel. What the hell do we do?"

"Climb down the ladder," Daniel commanded.

"Down the ladder?" Cam asked. "You mean with the sharks?"

"Not all the way down, just far enough so that the monster can't get us," Daniel said. "You go first, Cam. Then Abby and Annie. I'll follow behind. Keep the twins safe."

Cam nodded and started down the ladder. He could see the water below and knew the sharks were in it, but oddly enough, he wasn't even worrying about them. Three rungs above the water, Cam stopped.

"Okay, Annie and Abby climb down to me," Cam shouted. "Go slow. I'm right here waiting for you."

The twins hesitated.

"It's okay," Daniel assured the twins. "Just climb down to Cam. I'll be right behind you."

Abby and Annie nodded in unison and began climbing down. Daniel still couldn't tell them apart and had no idea which one went first.

Daniel watched the girls safely arrive at their brother. As Daniel placed his foot on the first rung of the ladder, the walls of the bell tower exploded in a shower of splinters, rain and wind.

Somewhere in the distance, Daniel could hear the dull clang of the church bell as it spiraled through the sky. The floor had dropped out from beneath Daniel. Gravity had lost its hold on him.

Rain and bits of splintered wood rained down into the church. Daniel could feel the debris peppering his face and arms. He reached out for the ladder, but only grabbed air. The panicked faces of Cam and the twins passed through Daniel's view before he splashed into the icy red water below.

-35-

Dubois kicked harder. He caught a glimpse of the three fins trailing behind him. Then there was a loud splash. Cal started screaming. Now a lone fin followed behind. Dubois hoped that Cal knew what he was doing.

The shark's nose bumped against the heel of Dubois' boot as he kicked and pulled himself through the cold salty water. There had been countless times that Dubois had watched sharks feed. Small fish were simply snapped up, but anything bigger needed to be prodded and tested. The shark was trying to figure out what he was and if he was edible. The shark turned and swam in a tight circle. The next pass was going to include a taste test.

Ray's clam boat bobbed in the small chop that was created between the buildings. Dubois was tired. Hell, he was tired when Ray pulled him from the ocean. Now he was fucking exhausted and had a shark swimming along behind him.

The hollow metallic *thunk* of Dubois' hand hitting the side of Ray's boat was about the most beautiful sound he could have imagined. Dubois got his elbow over the side of the boat and began pulling himself in. Every muscle burned, each fiber screaming in protest.

The shark completed its turn and came back for Dubois. Its torpedo like head cut through the water as it came in for the kill.

Dubois tumbled into the boat as the shark reared out of the water. The upper half of the animal slid into the boat behind Dubois and threatened to tip the boat. Water spilled in over the side. The clashing of row upon row of teeth rattled Dubois' bones. The boat rocked back and forth as the shark tried to force its sleek body further into the boat. Dubois, out of breath and exhausted, kicked out with both feet, striking the shark in the face and dumping it back into the water. It turned a quick circle beneath the boat, as if considering its options, and then swam back towards The Dry Dock and Cal.

Lungs burning and soaking wet, Dubois made his way to the steering wheel. In his rush to get to The Dry Dock, Ray had thankfully left the keys in the ignition. The red and white bobber on the keychain swung playfully as Dubois stumbled through the boat. Water splashed with each step, but the boat was still floating. People could bail the boat out with their hands once they were safely off the roof of the bar. Right now, all that mattered was getting the boat started.

Dubois turned the key. The engines whined in protest and Dubois had a moment of panic where he worried that water might have gotten into the fuel. Had this been for nothing? In a belch of black smoke and roar of mechanical fury, the engines came to life. Dubois pushed the throttle forward and swung the steering wheel in a tight circle.

Cal floated in the water in front of The Dry Dock. Ray and Big Mo screamed from the roof, but Dubois couldn't hear what they were saying over the wind. It didn't matter anyway. All that mattered was that Dubois got the boat to Cal before the sharks tore into him.

The boat shot past one shark, but two more had already closed in on Cal. Dubois gunned the engines and swung the boat around.

Cal felt the wake rock him back and could taste the acrid exhaust of the engines as they passed inches in front of him. A garbled sound mixed with the scream of the engines as the props bounced out of the water. The wake behind the boat turned red and bits of mangled shark floated past Cal.

"Come on! Come on," Dubois shouted as he put the throttle in neutral and rushed to pull Cal into the boat.

Cal swam towards the boat. Dubois had killed one or two sharks, but that still meant that at least one more was nearby. The blood and bits of chopped shark meat made it impossible to see what was beneath him in the water.

Grabbing Cal's hands, Dubois yanked him halfway into the boat.

"You crazy son of a bitch," Dubois panted. "What the hell were you thinking?"

"I had to buy you enough time to reach..." Cal's words were cut short as he was dragged beneath the water.

"Cal!" Dubois screamed and scanned the surrounding water.

A series of large bubbles dotted the red water and burst in rings of white foam.

"Cal!" Dubois screamed again. He felt helpless.

Two hands and then a head broke the surface. Dubois nearly dove from the boat to grab Cal's hands and pull him into the boat. Cal was silent, probably in shock.

"I got you. I got you," Dubois panted and gave one final pull to get Cal safely inside the boat.

Dubois' legs were warm. Blood spilled over Dubois' khaki uniform permanently staining it black. Cal's midsection was missing and a tangled knot of intestines and meat slapped against Dubois' thighs. Blood poured from the wound and mixed with the water in the bottom of the clam boat. Dubois flipped Cal onto his back and tried to stop the bleeding of a wound he knew was fatal. Two shaking fingers touched the side of Cal's neck to check for a pulse. Dubois couldn't process that Cal was dead. He had risked his life so Dubois could get to a fucking clam boat. Where was the sense in that? There was no pulse. The wind whipped against Dubois' legs. The blood turned cold and tacky. The fabric clung to his skin.

Dubois had pulled Cal into the boat, but it was too late. Cal was gone.

-36-

The world had gone dark and topsy-turvy after Daniel hit the water. In a moment of panic, he had sucked in a lungful of the revolting water. At least he hoped it was only water. Daniel's head broke the surface of the water. Lumps of meat bobbed in the ripples undulating near his neck. Daniel coughed and vomited a torrent of red water.

"Daniel, get out of the water," Cam shouted from the ladder. Daniel treaded water. Cam pointed towards the inky interior of the church. Abby and Annie looked on in terror. Daniel watched a series of small waves roll past his shoulders. Something was coming towards him.

"Swim," one of the twins yelled. A large fin rose in the water behind Daniel.

Looking behind would have been pointless. Daniel knew what was there. If it was one shark or fifty, it really didn't matter. One would be enough. Daniel kicked and pulled himself through the putrid water. An arm, ending in a severed stump, bumped his cheek. He tried to ignore the unsettling feeling of the raw, wet meat sliding across his face and continued towards the ladder.

Cam had come down as close to the water as the ladder would allow and reached out for Daniel.

"Come on," Cam shouted. "You're almost there. Keep going!"

Daniel felt his fingers brush a submerged rung of the ladder. He was exhausted. Cam reached down and grabbed the collar of Daniel's shirt. He yanked upwards, almost pulling the shirt over Daniel's head. Daniel kicked his feet, finding the submerged rung and pushed. Cam moved to the side of the ladder and pushed Daniel further up the ladder. Abby and Annie grabbed his shirt and pulled. Daniel climbed around the twins and wrapped his arms around the rungs of the ladder. Cam moved back up the ladder.

Daniel watched the shark bump against the ladder and then turn away. Its tail slapped against the ladder as the shark swam back towards the severed arm that had brushed against Daniel while he swam to safety. The shark snapped it jaws around the limb and dragged it beneath the water.

"Thank you," Daniel panted. His lungs burned and his body ached.

Cam looked up the ladder. A large hole hung above them. Rain and wind poured through the opening.

"You're welcome," Cam said. "But what now?"

"I don't know," Daniel shivered. Tears welled in his eyes. The other children couldn't tell if Daniel was crying or water dripped from his hair. No one would have blamed him for crying.

The remains of the bell tower floor groaned and snapped. Boards fell away and splashed into the water below.

"It's going to fall," one of the twins cried as a large chunk of wood sailed past them.

"Daniel, is it collapsing?" Cam yelled.

A scythe-like claw peeled away more wood, widening the opening so a second claw could find purchase in the old wood. Daniel could see the rough skin and scales that wrapped the claws. Each was easily the size of Daniel. The claws moved away and the roof of the church groaned and cracked.

"It's not collapsing. The dragon is on the roof," Daniel called shouted. "It's trying to get inside."

The opening at the top of the ladder was filled a huge yellow eye. Its diamond shaped iris contracted as the monster caught sight of the children. The eye disappeared.

Daniel hoped the dragon hadn't seen them or had lost interest. Maybe it found an easier meal.

The floor of the bell tower exploded as the claws split the old wood and forced their way further into the church.

-37-

Cal was a royal pain in the ass. No, Ray corrected himself. Cal had been a royal pain in the ass. Cal was dead. Still being a pain in the ass hardly excluded someone from being a good friend and that, Cal definitely had been.

The clam boat bobbed in the red water, water where Cal had moments before swam. Ray and Big Mo lowered people over the side of The Dry Dock and into the waiting boat. Dubois moved about, positioning people so that boat would remain balanced.

After the final person was lowered into the waiting boat, Big Mo turned and clasped Ray's shoulder.

"He was a good man," Big Mo said. "I'm gonna miss Cal, even if he was a pain in the ass."

"Me too," Ray nodded. Ray's father and grandfather had been close friends with Cal's family. So, much like everyone else on Sunset Island, Ray's best friend had been more of a family tradition as opposed to a decision. But that didn't make Cal any less of a good friend.

After Ray's marriage ended, half of Sunset Island was buzzing with gossip about lesbian affairs. Ray lost a good number of friends along with his wife. Sometimes that was just how things worked on Sunset Island, but not with Cal. He didn't care about why Ray's wife had left, only that she had and his friend needed support. Cal was like that. He knew all the gossip on the island, but he never really bought into it. Ray respected that about his friend. He would miss Cal, a lot of people on Sunset Island would. Of course, that was assuming that anyone was left on Sunset once this over.

"Come on, Ray," Big Mo motioned towards the boat. "We gotta get the lead outta our asses and get on over to the church."

"Agreed," Ray helped Big Mo into the boat. They were going to help whoever was in that church, even that grease ball of a mayor. That was why Cal gave his life. Ray would honor that.

"Ready?" Dubois asked.

"Move on over, son," Ray moved behind the steering wheel.

"I'm sorry about Cal," Dubois said. "I didn't know him long, but I could see he was a good man, probably a good friend too. I'm sorry that he had to trade his life for mine."

"He traded it for every life in this damn boat," Ray replied. "Don't beat yourself up. Cal knew what he was doing. We can be sad later. Right now, we gotta make sure what he did counts for something."

"Yeah," Dubois nodded. Ray could see that something was bothering the man, or at least something more than the obvious.

"What is it?" Ray asked. "Might as well as tell me now cuz I ain't gonna ask twice."

Dubois spat a wad of phlegm into the water. "It's the sharks."

"What about them?" Ray asked.

"Why are there so many here?" Dubois continued. "I'm sure you've had flooding here before and that the streets weren't filled with fucking sharks."

"That's true," Ray agreed. "My guess is that sea monster drove all them sharks towards the island. Can't imagine that thing is too picky when it comes to what it's eating. I think those sharks were running like the rest of us."

"Can't be sure it's a sea monster if it's on land, right?" Dubois laughed. His laughed was thin and forced.

Ray let a sad smile break across his face. "A wise man once said something like that." Ray turned to the people in the boat. "Everyone, hang on to something." Ray pushed the throttle forward.

Sharks swam through the streets of Sunset Island, but the noise of Ray's boat kept them away. A few would come close enough to panic people inside the boat, but Ray just motored past them.

Debris bobbed in the wake of Ray's boat. It was all trash now, but had once been important and treasured. These objects held memories. They defined lives. Like the keepsakes themselves, the people who had once cherished them would soon be forgotten.

The ocean had already reclaimed much of Sunset Island. The eaves of houses jutted above the dark water like broken teeth set into black gums. Ray knew the people that had called these houses home. Some were in his boat. Others went to the high school. Not many were left.

-38-

The dragon forced its snout through the opening above the ladder. Cam had already moved to just one rung above the water. Daniel and the twins moved down as well and pressed themselves against the ladder. The dragon pulled its face from the opening. Two sets of claws tore into the roof of the church as it tried to widen the space and find its way inside.

"Daniel, I don't see any sharks," Cam peered into the darkness of the church.

"It doesn't mean that they're not there," Daniel jumped to the other side of the ladder as a chunk of roofing sailed past his head. Shingles fluttered down between the raindrops.

"I think we're going to have to try to swim for it," Cam continued. "I bet the sharks are scared of the dragon too. You said it was sticking around here for food, right?"

"Yeah," Daniel answered. "But it was just a guess."

"I bet it would eat a shark if it had the chance," Cam added. "They left. They must have. I don't see any fins or waves or anything."

"Okay," Daniel said. "But where do we swim? We can't swim outside."

"There," Cam pointed towards the large white marble altar. The water had already made its way onto the platform, but the ceremonial center still stood above the red waves.

"Cam, you know we can't swim," one of the twins sniffled. "What are we going to do?"

"I'll take one of you and Daniel will take the other," Cam answered. "Just wrap your arms around our necks and don't let go. Keep your eyes closed and don't let go." The twin girls nodded.

"Let's g–" Daniel words were lost beneath an explosion of wood.

The dragon forced its scaly arm through the opening in the roof and swiped at the ladder, tearing it free from where it had been bolted to the bell tower floor. The ladder wobbled and then pitched forward. The dragon clawed for the ladder, but only succeeded in knocking it further into the church.

"Jump!" Cam leapt from the ladder. It hit the water with a loud slap and spray of foamy water. Cam felt his heart tighten as he broke the surface and saw no sign of his sisters.

Daniel knew they were going to fall. There was no avoiding that. He braced himself for impact and struggled out from underneath the ladder once it crashed into the water below. The twins had been closer to Daniel. They should be somewhere nearby. There was no sign of them.

Taking a deep breath, Daniel plunged back beneath the water. He forced his eyes open. The salt stung, but he needed to see. Blurry shadows and forms spread across the floor of the church. None moved. Daniel grabbed the nearest form and dragged it back to the surface.

The man in the linen suit glared at Daniel with one dead eye. What remained of his face was frozen in a look of pure terror. Daniel cried out and pushed the torso away from him. It gently bumped against the ladder, both linen and skin fluttering in the water.

Daniel dove back beneath the water. Two small forms struggled to free themselves from under something. Daniel kicked harder and grabbed the girls by the collars of their t-shirts. Bracing against the floor, Daniel pushed and kicked upwards with all the force he could summon. He broke the surface with Abby in one hand and Annie in the other, though he couldn't tell which was in what hand.

The twins coughed and spat salt water, but they were alive. Cam swam up next to Daniel. He had lost sight of the other children for what couldn't have been longer than thirty to forty seconds, but the moment had felt stretched and distorted to excruciating lengths.

"Help me get them up here." Daniel pushed one of the twins onto a nearby pew that floated atop the water. Cam hefted the second girl up beside her sister.

"Are you okay?" Cam asked. The twins nodded and coughed.

"We were stuck," Annie said.

"And Daniel saved us," Abby added, finishing the sentence.

Cam turned to Daniel. "Thanks."

A fin pierced the water and cut towards the children. Waves rode forward on the shark's momentum.

"Get up there," Daniel shouted and pushed Cam towards the pew. Cam scrambled onto the heavy wooden bench. It began to sink under the icy water.

"It won't hold me," Cam cried. "It won't hold you."

"Abby. Annie. We need to go right now," Daniel said. "Come on. Right now."

The girls hesitated.

"I didn't let anything happen to you before and I won't now. Jump in the water. We need to swim now," Daniel commanded. Tears streaked down the twins' faces, but they listened and slid off the pew into the water.

The twins clung to the pew like the edge of a pool.

"Let go," Cam tugged one of the twins away. "We've got you."

Daniel and Cam swam towards the altar, each with a twin clinging to their necks. Abby or Annie, whichever one was on Daniel's back, opened her eyes and looked behind.

"Shark," the twin shrieked. She kicked her feet against Daniel's waist, as if willing him to swim faster.

The shark's head rose out of the water as it prepared to tear a chunk of meat from Daniel.

A section of roof the size of a small car splashed into the water behind the shark. The startled animal turned to investigate the disturbance. The dragon's clawed hand shot through the opening, spearing the shark through its back and plucking it from the water. As lightning flashed, Daniel saw the dragon close its jaws around half of the shark. It tore away the head and fins. The tail, clutched between claws, thrashed a few more times before the dragon consumed it.

Cam helped Daniel and the twin onto the altar. Water lapped at the edges of the ornate stone table. They would be safe, at least from the sharks.

Wind and rain whipped through the openings in the church roof. The dragon peered into the darkness below, trying to find its escaped prey.

A burst of red light illuminated the sky, blinding the children.

"What's happening?" one of the twins cried.

"Is it breathing fire?" the other one whimpered.

"Lay down," Daniel barked at the other children. Spots of glittering red danced through his vision. He wanted to tell the twins that the dragon wasn't breathing fire. That it would be impossible. That the dragon's mouth wasn't glowing red and shooting sparks. But Daniel didn't want to lie to them either.

Daniel and Cam didn't know if it really was a dragon, but it sure looked like one. And one thing everyone knew about dragons was that they breathed fire.

-39-

The church bell hadn't rung since Ray started driving the boat towards the old white building. But that didn't mean that the people were gone or in any less need of help.

"On the roof," Dubois shouted from the bow of the boat. He pointed towards the church. A long shadow crept up the side of the church and slithered along the roof of the church, tearing away sections with each step. The monster's rear legs still stood in the water as its upper half reached into the church.

"At least we know where it is," Big Mo shrugged.

"And it wouldn't be here if no one was inside," Ray yelled over the engine. He had stopped the boat by the high school and let the passengers climb onto the roof of the building. There was little room left in the boat and whoever was in church was going to need it. A small maintenance shed on the roof would provide shelter from the wind and rain. As long as they stayed quiet, the monster should leave them alone. Big Mo and Dubois insisted on accompanying Ray to the church. He wanted them out of harm's way, but was glad to have them along with him.

"Well, what do we do now?" Big Mo asked.

"Ray, this clam boat is a flat bottom, right?" Dubois asked. He moved towards the back of the boat.

"Wouldn't be a clam boat if it wasn't," Ray answered. "Why?"

"I don't think anyone is going to be able to make it outside with that fucking dinosaur on the roof. So maybe we should go to them," Dubois said.

Ray thought about it for a moment. "The water is probably deep enough that we can drive the boat right into the church. The hull will clear the steps no problem, but we'd wreck the props. We're screwed if the engines are shot."

"Big Mo, help me out," Dubois pointed towards the twin engines on the stern of Ray's boat. He pulled the levers to unlock the engines. Big Mo moved beside Dubois. "Ray, gun it to the front doors. When you hit the stairs, we'll pull the engines up."

The monster turned towards the boat, attracted to the roar of the engines. It prepared to drop from the roof and pursue an easier meal.

"Shit it knows we're here," Dubois groaned.

"Didn't think it would notice two big ass engines making a whole lotta noise?" Big Mo laughed. "Dubois, if you ain't a glass half full kinda guy, I don't know who is."

"Here," Ray held out an orange gun with an oversized barrel.

"A flare gun?" Big Mo asked. "Shit, Ray, maybe you're the one that's full of pointless hopes and dreams and not Dubois. What the hell are we going to do with that thing besides piss the monster off?"

"It's chewing," Ray answered. "Next time it opens its mouth, shoot it."

"I'll do it," Dubois held out his hand.

"No offense, son," Ray said, "but I'd be a hell of a lot more comfortable with that thing in Big Mo's hands."

"I was on the rifle squad in high school," Big Mo explained. "I even got a varsity letter."

"What the hell does color guard and twirling fake rifles have to do with shooting that thing in the mouth?" Dubois argued. "I handled guns all the time."

"Do I look like I had a ton of school spirit?" Big Mo laughed. "It wasn't no color guard, you asshole. It was shooting. I was best in the state."

"Okay, fine," Dubois relented. "Just shoot the fucking thing already."

Ray gunned the engines and the boat lurched forward. Big Mo steadied herself and watched as the monster opened its mouth to eat what looked like the lower half of a shark. She took in a deep breath, let out half and squeezed the trigger. A loud *POP* and acrid cloud of smoke filled the air. A small comet streaked towards the creature and sailed between its massive jaws and into its mouth.

"Holy shit," Dubois cheered. "Nice shot. I apologize."

"Accepted," Big Mo nodded. "Now grab the damn engine."

The monster reared its head back. A deep red glow shone in its throat and sparks shot from between its lips. Big Mo wondered if she had gotten the flare lodged between two of the monster's teeth.

With a loud splash, the monster dropped from the roof of the church and retreated towards the cemetery.

The bow of the boat bumped on the stairs. Dubois and Big Mo pulled the engines out of the water and let momentum carry them inside. The props spun wildly as the engine belched exhaust.

"Drop them back in," Ray yelled. The last thing he wanted to do was wait around for that thing to come back.

Four children stared wide-eyed as Ray drove the clam boat up the aisle of the church. He pulled the throttle back and glided to the altar.

"You four all that's left?" Ray asked the kids. They nodded. "Time to go, kids."

Big Mo and Dubois helped the four children into the boat. They looked scared and a little banged up, but otherwise okay.

Once the kids were seated, Ray spun the wheel and gunned the engine. "Get ready back there," Ray yelled to Dubois and Big Mo.

The bow of the boat cleared the doors of the church when the rear wall of the building collapsed. The creature pushed aside stone and wood as it clawed its way into the church. The remaining walls trembled and threatened to fall as the monster stormed down the center of the church towards the boat.

"It's the dragon," one of the kids screamed. Ray didn't think the creature was an actual dragon, but thought the description was pretty spot on. Hell, maybe it was a fucking dragon, for all he knew.

"Pull the engines up," Ray yelled. The boat thudded and metal screeched. The engines bounced and splashed back into the water. Ray knew the props had hit the stone steps. He had heard that noise once before. Granted, when it happened before, Ray had been drunk and drove his boat into shallow water, not through a church with a damn dragon behind him.

The boat pulled to the side and drove funny, but still drove. Ray could worry about nautical maintenance later. The boat still drove, that was all that mattered.

The monster exploded from the front of the church, completely demolishing the building. It dropped to its belly and slithered through the water in wide S curves.

Ray opened the throttle up completely. He was pushing the boat to its limit, but figured if he didn't, he wouldn't be around to care that his boat still worked. The creature, a dragon or whatever it was, was gaining on them.

"There," one of the kids yelled and pointed towards the decorative stone arch that bridged Spruce Avenue. Ray had voted against Mayor Billings spending taxpayer money on building that stupid thing and commemorating whatever he was out to commemorate. At the time, Ray had wondered why did anything or anyone need a two story high pile of rocks to be remembered. But right now, it was beautiful.

"Everybody duck," Big Mo yelled as the boat shot under the stone arch. Metal screeched and things fell away as the boat pushed further under the arch. There was barely enough room for the adults to crouch and children to sit up.

The monster's claw probed the space under the arch, but couldn't find the boat. The arch shook as the creature tried to collapse the structure. Bits of mortar and small stones rained down onto the boat and its occupants. It held strong.

"Shit," Big Mo laughed, "that Billings was one crooked son of a bitch, but right about now, I'd kiss his big ol' ass."

"Like my day wasn't bad enough?" Ray snorted. "Now I got that mental picture haunting me too."

"You're welcome," Big Mo grinned.

-40-

Hibernating for so long had left the creature near starving. Its old hunting grounds, once plentiful with fish were now barren, though it had found a suitable substitute. The creature by nature protested leaving the deep water, but its hunger demanded that it go where the food was.

The hunting grounds had been bountiful and rising water made the hunt easier, but food was becoming scarcer and more problematic to obtain. A few more meals and the creature could return to its slumber.

Turning away from where the last bit of food had disappeared, the creature flicked its tongue and scented the air. There was still food to be found in these hunting grounds. Dropping to its belly, the creature slithered through the water.

The abundant scent of food whipped about on the turbulent storm winds. The creature could still track the scent. It had hunted here before, but the creature must have missed some food.

Pulling itself out of the water, the creature stalked its prey. With a lightning fast snap of its jaws, the creature found food.

Food scattered from where it hid, but didn't make it very far. The creature was fast.

Bits of meat, too small to be concerned with, fell to the ground and were crushed beneath the creature's massive claws.

More food moved off the side. The creature swept its spiked tail, knocking some food into the water for later and trapping others for right now. The creature gorged on easy prey.

The prey was afraid and making it easy to catch. The creature enjoyed the hunt, savored a well-earned meal, but would never pass up the chance to fill its belly. Soon these hunting grounds would be barren and the creature could return to its slumber.

Until then, the creature would hunt. Hunt and feed.

-41-

"I think the dragon is gone. We should go now," the young boy named Daniel said. Ray could see that the boy had become something of a leader for the other children. It made Ray shudder to think about what they must have gone through and what they must have seen.

Everyone introduced themselves while they waited under the stone arch. The water was still rising and sooner, rather than later, they would have to leave or become stuck.

"What makes you think it's a dragon?" Big Mo asked.

"What makes you so sure it's not?" Cam retorted. "It was going to breathe fire back at the church. I'd say that makes it a dragon."

"Kid, it wasn't breathing fire," Big Mo laughed. "It was trying to get inside the church, so I shot that damn thing in the mouth with an emergency flare."

"Oh," Cam looked oddly disappointed. "Well, it still could be a dragon, though."

"Shit kid," Big Mo snorted, "it could be a dinosaur or a sea monster or who knows what else. Might as well be a dragon too, right?"

Cam let out a small laugh.

"It's time to get a move on," Ray peered out through the opening between the water line and top of the arch. Ray crawled to the back of the boat and glimpsed at the props beneath the water. He couldn't inspect them as much as he would have liked, but what he could see told him enough. "We got a problem. The stone stairs chewed the props to shit. There's no way this boat is making it through storm waves."

"It wouldn't have held the others anyway," Dubois said. "We're going to need something bigger."

"He's right, Ray," Big Mo added. "I'm guessing that the plan is to grab the others and get the hell off of Sunset. This boat loaded with people would get flipped over or swamped by a storm wave."

"Getting to the mainland is our best bet," Ray agreed. "But you're both right. We need a bigger boat."

"It's too bad that the monster already sunk the ferry," Dubois said.

"Dragon," Cam cut in.

"Yeah, sorry," Dubois nodded. "The dragon already sunk the ferry. That's probably the biggest boat on the island."

"Still wouldn't be big enough," Ray said. "That thing sunk your cargo ship like it was little more than a dingy."

"So what's that mean?" Daniel asked.

"It means we're going to need two boats," Ray answered. "We're going to need to divide the...uh, the dragon's attention."

"Okay," Dubois said, "but we still need bigger boats to make it off the island."

"I know where we can get them," Ray said. "The town boatyard is in the middle of the island. There are a bunch of boats there in dry dock that should still be okay."

"Anything big enough?" Dubois asked

"There's two old ferryboats in dry dock," Ray answered. "Mayor Billings had them taken out of the fleet a few months ago."

"Is there anything wrong with them?" Big Mo asked.

"No, I think that bastard just wanted to make the ferry lines longer, so the island looked more popular. The boats look like rusted hunks of shit and everyone is probably gonna get tetanus from them, but they'll float and the engines should still work," Ray said. "They'll need to be fueled, but there should be something at the boatyard we can use."

"Alright," Big Mo nodded, "A little bit of rust ain't nothing to worry about. If them turds will float, I say we go for it."

"Agreed," Dubois said. "But what are we going to do about the people we left on the roof of the high school?"

"You think you can handle getting the ferryboats fueled and running?" Ray asked Dubois. "They got big diesel engines, nothing that should give you any trouble. Sure as hell aren't as complicated as what you had on that big old cargo ship."

"I can figure it out," Dubois said. "And what I don't know, I'll make up."

"You take Big Mo and the kids with you," Ray said. "I'll drop all of you at the boatyard and then go get those people off the roof of the high school."

Ray started the boat. He half expected the monster's scaly claw to begin swiping for them again, but nothing happened. The boat rumbled out from under the stone arch. The rain and wind once again began to beat against the boat and passengers.

A dark lump, vaguely in the shape of the lower half of a human drifted just beneath the surface. Ray looked over the side of the boat. The shoes still tied to the severed legs looked familiar. It was probably someone Ray had called a friend or neighbor. He was quickly running out of both.

"Let's go," Ray turned away from the ragged remains and headed towards the boatyard.

-42-

The Sunset Island Boatyard stood in the middle of the island. It was situated on one side of a large rise. The town dump sat on the other side. Storm surges had already reached the dump and flooded the nearby water with cans from the recycling center and large bags of trash that fluttered beneath the surface looked like huge jellyfish.

Ray pulled the throttle back and carefully picked his way through the field of debris. The last thing he needed was to waste time untangling a knot of shredded plastic from one of the propellers. Cam and Daniel stood in the bow of the boat and pushed aside trash with oars as the boat chugged forward. Big Mo sat on the middle bench with the twins Abby and Annie. Ray still had no idea which one was which. Dubois scanned the area for sharks or the monster. Both were thankfully absent.

Swinging the boat around the perimeter of the town dump, Ray caught sight of the boatyard. The fence leading into the boatyard stood open. Ray didn't know if it was the water or someone's carelessness that left it open and honestly didn't care. He guided the clam boat deeper into the boatyard.

A small restaurant sat on the pier. The windows had been smashed by the storm and garbage from the nearby dump. The storm surge piled overturned tables and chairs against the bar. Ray had only been in the boatyard bar for a few drinks, but it still made him sad to see it destroyed. It was just another piece of Ray's world slipping under the waves.

"Over there," Dubois pointed to where the two hulking ferryboats sat on risers. The water had almost reached the hulls. All they would need to do is get the boats fueled and off the blocks.

"Here," Ray passed a coil of rope to Dubois. "Wrap this around one of the blocks and I'll pull it free. Once we yank one, the ferry should do the rest of the work for us."

Dubois leapt out of the boat and waded through the chest deep water. He secured the rope around one of the blocks and passed the end to Big Mo who tied it off on one of cleats on the stern of Ray's clam boat.

"Watch yourself," Ray yelled as he gunned the engine. The boat strained and then lurched forward as the block came free. The ferry groaned, tilted to the side and splashed into the water. They repeated the process with the second ferry.

"Well, at least they float," Big Mo said.

"Big Mo," Ray said, "take the kids on the first ferry. Get them inside and outta this rain. Then you and Dubois drop the ramp on the second one. I'm going to look into getting us some gas." Big Mo nodded and leapt out of the clam boat. She and Dubois helped the children onto one of the ferries and then went about dropping the ramps into the water. "Dubois, take the rope and lash the boats together. We won't have much reach with the fuel hose, but it should be long enough if the boats are close. Get 'em tied up and then look for a round panel in the deck. That'll be where the fuel goes."

"Got it," Dubois waved. He tied the rope off on one ferry and tossed it onto the deck of the other. Dubois jumped into the water and waded over to the second ferry. He grabbed the line and began lashing the boats together.

Ray motored towards the garage. The garage looked like an old airplane hangar. The curved metal exterior had long ago become rusted and pitted. Two sliding barn doors hung to the side, partially off their tracks. A large pickup truck with a gas tank on the back sat in water. Ray cut the throttle back and climbed out of the boat. Grabbing a hammer from a tool bench, Ray climbed onto the truck's running board and smashed the window. He stuck his hand through the shattered window and pulled the door handle.

Noticing that the door had been unlocked, Ray let out a laugh. "Probably should'a tried the handle first. Guess you don't get to smash a window every day, so what the hell?"

There were keys in the truck, but Ray doubted the engine would kick over with all the salt water in it. All he really wanted to be sure of was that the battery still had a charge. The tires were large enough that the battery should be safely out of the salt water. If it was dead, so were they. The dome light in the ceiling of the truck came on and Ray grinned. Sometimes, things worked when they should.

After shifting the truck into neutral and releasing the parking brake, Ray climbed out of the cab and waded around to the front bumper. A large winch was bolted onto the bumper in front of the grill. Ray pulled the release and unspooled the rusted cable. He wrapped the cable around the cleats on the rear of his boat and locked the hook in place. Returning to the winch, Ray locked the reel in place.

The truck protested, but the twin engines of Ray's clam boat eventually pulled it free from the garage. It was slow going, but Ray got the truck lined up with one of the ferry's ramps.

Ray cut the engine and climbed out of his boat again. Freeing the winch line, Ray passed it to Dubois, who then hooked to one of the oversized cleats on the bow of the ferry. Ray climbed back into the cab of the truck and flicked the button to reel in the winch. The pickup truck slowly pulled itself up the ramp and onto the ferry. Ray turned the truck off and jumped out.

"Get both ferryboats fueled and ready to go," Ray said to Dubois.

"What about the keys?" Dubois asked.

"Taped under the captain's chair in each cabin," Ray grinned. "Some days, my head was a bit fuzzy and I'd forget to bring the keys from home, so I hid one under the seat in every ferry. They should still be there."

"Praise God for hangovers," Dubois laughed.

"It's about time they were good for something," Ray said. He helped Dubois close the ramp to each ferry and pulled himself back into the clam boat. "Be ready to go as soon as I get back. There ain't many people left on Sunset, so I'm guessing I know where that damn dragon might be and I don't want to be screwing around if it's chasing after us."

"Are there any weapons around here?" Dubois looked towards the flooded buildings that were scattered around the island boatyard.

"I dunno," Ray answered. "There might be a shotgun or pistol or something around here. Nothing that would do anything to that monster beyond piss it off. And I'm pretty sure that there ain't any bazookas squirreled away."

"I guess you're right," Dubois said. "I'd just feel better about you heading over to that school if you had a weapon."

"Hell," Ray waved the flare gun, "I got this right here and a bad attitude. We'll see how far that can get me." Ray tucked the flare gun into his belt. He knew it wouldn't do anything to the creature. Big Mo's shot had been one in a million and Ray wasn't looking to try his luck. But it was better than nothing.

"Alright," Dubois relented. "Just be careful."

"Will do," Ray nodded. "Now stop mothering me and get them fucking ferryboats fueled up."

Dubois climbed onto the side of one ferry and leapt onto the deck of the other. The fuel tank on the back of the truck had a hand crank, which was a stroke of luck, but also meant it would take a long time to fuel the boats. Dubois got to work.

Big Mo and the children were inside one of the narrow passenger cabins. The interior was little more than a long wooden bench and a few round windows, but all were glad to be out of the storm and finally somewhere dry. Big Mo glanced out the windows and saw Ray and Dubois had gotten the fuel truck on board.

"Ray," Big Mo shut the door of the passenger cabin behind her. The kids were settled into the passenger cabin.

"What is it?" Ray asked.

"If that thing is already at the high school," Big Mo paused, "then there ain't no reason for you to go back there. Those people are gone, Ray. You and I both know that to be the truth."

"I dropped those people off and promised I'd come back," Ray said. "I gotta at least try. Even if it's already too late."

Ray gunned the clam boat's engines and headed towards the high school.

-43-

The half sunken remains of a fishing boat sat in the middle of an intersection. Ray swung his clam boat around the wreck and headed towards the island golf course. He had never been one to waste a good day chasing some little ball around, not when there was drinking to be done, but the golf course would give him a clear path to the high school.

The clubhouse sat at the top of a steep incline that marked the end of the eighteenth hole. It looked like an island. Ray slowed the engine and carefully edged around the building. Fear of a submerged car or golf cart kept him from motoring at full throttle. The hull of the clam boat screeched as it passed over some submerged wreckage. A hard turn of the steering wheel and it was free. Ray looked into the choppy water, but couldn't find what he had hit.

Images of the sea monster coming up from under the water and snapping up the boat flooded Ray's mind. He shook his head and pushed the ideas to the side. There was no way that thing was lying in wait on the golf course. The hills were steep on the sides of the course and the water wasn't deep enough to hide a lizard the size of cargo ship.

"Stupid," Ray muttered to himself. He was letting his fear get the better of him.

A narrow gravel road wound away from the clubhouse and towards the high school. Ray imagined that the road would look more like a riverbed than a path at this point. The tops of the surrounding trees blew in the gusting wind and dipped into the water. Ray was grateful for the coverage they provided.

The high school loomed off to the left of the path. It wasn't a large building, as far as high schools went, but it never needed to be. The population of Sunset Island had been declining for a few years and class sizes shrank with it. Ray figured that once this was over the island might not even need a school anyone, let alone a high school. But that was of course assuming that anyone was left to worry about those kinds of details.

Ray motored towards the high school. He searched the roof for the outline of the maintenance shed on the roof. It was gone. No one cried out for help or ran towards the sound of his boat's engines. Ray pulled up alongside the roof and checked anyway. Maybe some were injured and needed help. Maybe they were hiding.

Remains of both the maintenance shed and survivors littered the roof. Ray tried not to focus on the chewed limbs and ragged hunks of meat. He tried not to stare into the large red puddles that slowly crept towards one another. He failed.

Ray put these people here. He had promised they would be safe. He was supposed to come back and take them to safety. Instead, he had left them stranded. He had left them as a buffet for that fucking sea dragon.

The clam boat rocked in the water, a series of swells passing under the boat. As Ray rode the swells up, he caught a glimpse of the other side of the high school. The monster glared back at him, its head and one claw resting on a lower section of the roof. The creature tilted its head, as if unsure why food would be staring at it instead of running. Ray watched ripples pass over the scaly muscles of the dragon's neck and shoulder as it uncurled its lithe body from around the submerged high school and dropped into the water.

Swinging the steering wheel and gunning the engine, Ray pointed the clam boat back towards the Sunset Island Boatyard. The engines groaned in mechanical protest, coughing clouds of gray smoke before sputtering to a stop.

"Shit. Shit. Shit," Ray yelled as he turned the key in the ignition. There was no point. He had pushed the boat too hard and now it was dead. Ray figured the same could be said about him, because soon enough he would be too.

-44-

"Where are you going?" Dubois yelled from the control tower of the ferry. The kids looked out from the passenger cabin. Big Mo had paced from one end of the deck to the other and leapt over the side into the water.

"I'm going over the office and finding some keys," Big Mo shouted back to Dubois as she treaded water.

"Keys?" Dubois asked. "I found the keys for both boats right where Ray said they'd be. We don't need the keys."

"Not for the boats," Big Mo answered. "Ray has been gone too long. Something is wrong. I'm gonna find keys to something and go get his stupid ass."

"Come back," Dubois said. "I'll go look for Ray. You stay here with the kids."

"Ain't you a chivalrous one?" Big Mo laughed. "Nope, you're staying out. You and Ray are the only ones that know how to drive these ferries, so I'm the only one that can leave to find him. If I'm not back in thirty minutes, I want you and them kids gone. Got it?"

"But," Dubois began to argue.

"Got it?" Big Mo repeated.

"Yeah," Dubois nodded. "Just be careful." He was getting tired of telling people to be careful when there was clearly no way they could.

Big Mo continued swimming towards the boatyard office. The door was shut and the windows were broken. Water slipped in around the door, but she could see the box bolted to the back wall that held keys. An old post that had once been part of a farm fence near the pier floated by. Big Mo grabbed it and thrust the post through the window. Water gushed through the opening. Big Mo kicked against the current, not wanting to swim through broken glass.

Once the water had calmed, Big Mo used the post to knock away the rest of the glass. She swam into the office, banging her knee on the desk that sat under the broken window.

The key box was unlocked. No one every really worried about things getting stolen on Sunset Island. Sometimes the ferry folk would get a little rowdy, but locking doors was something that you just didn't do on Sunset Island. A few sets of keys dangled from hooks, but the ones at the end of a yellow curl of plastic caught Big Mo's attention.

Big Mo had grown up around boats, but that was never really her first choice of watercraft. Years ago, she had taken a rare vacation in the Playa Riviera. A week spent drinking tequila and tooling around Mexican beaches on a Jet Ski and she was hooked. She grabbed the key and strapped the Velcro bracelet to her wrist.

The lot number for the Jet Ski said it was somewhere behind the office. Big Mo swam outside and around the back of the office. A blue tarp sat on a small trailer beneath the water. Its familiar shape told Big Mo all she needed to know. She took a deep breath and dove under. Big Mo pulled the tarp free and returned to surface for air. She took in another breath and dove under to release the cables holding the Jet Ski to the trailer.

The Jet Ski floated to the surface. It had been underwater, but Big Mo figured it would still run. She had damn near sunk that Mexican one when she was bombed on margaritas and trying to see if she could drive the damn thing onto a dock. Those things were made to go underwater and be fine.

Big Mo pulled herself onto the Jet Ski. She clipped the key into place and pushed the button to start the engine. The Jet Ski sputtered and protested, but kicked over on the fourth try.

The children and Dubois looked on with worried expressions as Big Mo rocketed past the ferries on the Jet Ski. She let out a loud laugh and waved. Big Mo planned on coming back, but just in case, she made sure to look happy. The last thing she wanted was to leave the kids with a sad memory. They had enough of those already.

-45-

Death came for all men. Ray accepted this fact long before he accepted the existence of sea monsters or dragons or whatever it was that was going to kill him. The engine had been ripped off the back of the clam boat as if they were little more than a hangnail.

Ray watched the water spill in, flooding the stern of the boat. He rushed to the bow of the boat and braced himself as it titled up and began sinking. A swell moved through the water towards the clam boat. Ray figured there were two choices – stay in the boat and probably die or swim for it.

The water was cold, colder than Ray thought it should have been, but storms could do that. Ray kicked and swam, for what, he didn't know. The town was destroyed and half underwater. The high school was nearby, but that was where the monster had come from, so there was no point swimming towards there. At best, Ray was fighting to add a few meaningless seconds to his life, and draw a few more breaths before the dragon snapped him out of the water.

Metal screeched as the creature's jaws folded the aluminum of the boat in on itself. Rows of teeth shredded the metal. The monster flicked its serpentine neck and tossed the ruined hull of the boat over the roof of the high school.

Ray heard the splash and kept kicking. There had to be somewhere to hide, somewhere to escape death. The crown of a tree whipped about in the wind. Most of it was underwater, but the branches still stretched and tried to break free from the salt water. Grabbing the branch, Ray pulled himself out of the water. He doubted that the tree would offer him much protection. It was better than staying in the water. At least this way, Ray could see death coming for him.

The dragon swam past the tree. It was just beneath the surface. Ray watched the iridescent scales on the creature's back shimmer as it snaked its way past the tree. It would be back.

The wind howled as it slipped through the skeletal branches of the tree and rattled the leaves. Ray shivered and climbed higher. The branches creaked. Too much higher and the limbs would snap.

Something growled in the distance. Ray looked, trying to find the source of the sound. He didn't remember the monster making any noise. Maybe it had and Ray missed it.

A spray of water splashed through the leaves of the tree. Salty foam rained down on Ray's head and face, making his eyes sting. Ray let go of the branch with one hand and rubbed his eyes. Was the monster screwing with him before it ate him?

"Come on," Big Mo said as she made a second pass on the jet ski. "Get your ass outta that tree."

"Big Mo, what the hell are you doing here?" Ray asked and began climbing out of the tree.

"Saving your ass by the looks of it," Big Mo answered. "Now come on before that god damn dragon comes back."

Ray splashed into the water and swam towards Big Mo and her jet ski. The wind and water pushed the small craft further away and Ray struggled to close the distance.

I'm swimming around in fucking work boots. Cut me a break, Mother Nature. Ray thought.

Big Mo waved for Ray to hurry. She was blind to what rose from the water behind her.

"Big Mo," Ray shouted. He tried to point to warn his friend.

Water cascaded around Big Mo. She looked up and stared into a chasm lined with nests of crooked teeth. The creature's fetid breath washed over Big Mo. It stank of decay, the decay of people she had once known and called friends. A string of curse words flooded Big Mo's mind. The words jumbled together and were lost. She wanted to curse the monster, and yell something witty or inspiring for Ray.

Big Mo managed to raise her middle finger.

The bone on bone clash of countless of teeth gnashing together made Ray's ears ring. Blood splashed across the seat of the Jet Ski. Big Mo was gone.

-46-

Thirty minutes passed faster than Dubois would have liked. After the monster destroyed the *Ponce De Leon,* time had stretched and yawned. Now that Dubois needed a few extra minutes, it sped up. Fate or God or whoever was in control had a strange sense of humor.

Dubois wanted to wait. He wanted to believe that Big Mo and Ray would be back. But he couldn't lie to himself and more importantly, he couldn't lie to the kids. If Dubois had been alone, he would have waited. As it was, he was not alone. He was responsible for these kids, for their safety and that meant leaving.

The heavy diesel engine of the ferry rumbled to life, belching black smoke into the air. Dubois checked the gauges on the control panel. Everything looked in working order. The engine growled and shook as Dubois got the ferry moving. They were going forward, but the progress was slow.

"Shit," Dubois said as he looked out the window and realized that he forgot to untie the other ferry. He half walked and half slid down the metal stairs onto the deck of the ferry.

"What's wrong?" Daniel asked. He left the other children in the passenger cabin and joined Dubois on the deck.

"It's time to go," Dubois said as he untied the heavy ropes that lashed the two boats together. He tossed the coil of rope onto the deck of the other ferry.

"What about Ray and Big Mo?" Daniel asked. "We can't leave without them."

"I don't like it anymore than you do, kid," Dubois said, "but we can't wait around any longer. Big Mo said after thirty minutes we were supposed to head out, so that's what we're going to do."

"But what if they come back and we're not here?" Daniel continued.

"I gassed the other ferry up and checked over the controls," Dubois said. "If they come back, then the boat will be waiting for them. Like I said, kid, I don't like this anymore than you do, but I have to make sure that the three of you are safe. That's what's most important. Ray and Big Mo would agree. Head back into the cabin and let the other kids know that we're moving out."

Daniel nodded and walked back to the cabin. Dubois could see him relaying the message to the other children. They looked upset.

Dubois tired not to make eye contact with the children as he made his way back to the controls.

-47-

Ray swam for the Jet Ski, not that he wanted to. There just was nowhere left to go. Swimming back to the tree would only delay the inevitable. The only possible avenue of escape was on that Jet Ski.

The dragon dove beneath the water after it ate Big Mo. Ray watched it glide through the water and around the back of the high school. It would be back once it was done with its meal.

The white sides of the Jet Ski were splashed with a wild red design. Ray climbed onto the back of the vehicle and gagged as his feet bumped against Big Mo's boots, which still sat on the running boards. A ragged stump of meat peaked out from the tops of the boots. Ray used the toe of his foot to push Big Mo's boots into the water. It felt wrong, somehow disrespectful to dispose of what little remained of his friend in such a manner, but Ray couldn't stomach the idea of keeping the boots on the Jet Ski with him.

Big Mo's blood made the fake leather seat on the Jet Ski slippery. Ray slid forward, trying not the think about what lubricated his motion.

"Where's the fucking key?" Ray searched area. A middle finger waved at Ray from the water.

The lower section of Big Mo's arm drifted alongside the Jet Ski with its middle finger still defiantly raised. The Velcro safety bracelet and key were still strapped around the stump of Big Mo's arm.

Ray couldn't help but smirk when he saw Big Mo's middle finger. Even death couldn't stop Big Mo from being Big Mo. The smile faded from Ray's face when he realized that he was going to have to touch the severed remains of his friend's arm.

Grabbing the yellow curl of plastic, Ray fished Big Mo's forearm from the water. A splintered edge of bone jutted from the ruined limb. Ray tried not to look at it. Closing his eyes, Ray tried to release the safety bracelet.

A loud splash sounded off to the side of the Jet Ski.

Ray dropped Big Mo's severed arm into his lap and clicked the key into place. He tried to ignore the scratching of the exposed bone against his jeans.

A rooster tail of water erupted from the back of the Jet Ski as Ray swung it around in a tight circle and headed for the boatyard. He didn't need to look behind him to know that the monster was close behind.

-48-

Dubois guided the ferry towards open water. Huge, dark swells of water threatened to swallow the craft, but Dubois had steered more than his share of ships through a storm. His stomach rose and fell with the waves, giving the sensation of a rollercoaster, but none of the fun. Dubois hoped the kids were holding on to something.

A wave broke across the front of the ferry and the deck disappeared under the wash of stormy water. A second wave battered the ship from the side. Dubois would need to be careful. Too many waves like the last one and they could be flipped or swamped. The ferry was a tank as far as ships were concerned, but that didn't mean shit if salt water swamped the engine. Then it would only be a matter of time before they sank.

Exhaust plumed from the ferry's smoke stack as Dubois gunned the engine and drove the ship up the glassy face of an oncoming wave. The ferry broke through the lip of the wave and sped down into the trough. More waves were coming. Dubois couldn't help but think of a washing machine.

Lightning flashed and the water shone like obsidian. Dubois looked out the rear window towards Sunset Island. The remains of the island cut through the turbulent storm waters like the humped backs of massive whales. The ferry had been embattled from the get go and Dubois hadn't made it as far as he would have liked. A second set of lightning illuminated the velvety sky, painting Sunset Island in a blinding flash of blue electricity. That was when Dubois saw it.

A huge shadow, its back ridged with crooked spikes, loomed on the edge of Sunset Island. It whipped its head about in the storm. The monster loomed on the edge of the island and Dubois hoped it would stay there, that it wouldn't be able to see the ferry amongst all of the choppy storm waves.

As it dove into the inky water, Dubois knew his hopes had been misplaced. The monster was coming for the ferry and there was no way they would be able to outrun it.

-49-

Ray swung the Jet Ski into the boatyard. One of the ferries was gone. He felt a strange mix of emotions at seeing the boat gone. On one hand, he was glad that Dubois had gotten those kids off of Sunset, but on the other, Ray was alone.

Alone? Ray wondered. How the hell was he alone? At the very least, the sea monster should have been behind him. It had been right behind him since the high school. Now it was oddly missing.

A bright flash of lightning illuminated the ocean. Ray watched the ferry chug its way over the crest of a large storm swell and disappear in the trough of the next. A dark shape speared through the next set of waves and followed the same path as the ferry. The monster was going after a bigger meal.

Pulling the Jet Ski alongside the remaining ferry, Ray jumped up from the seat. Ray's jeans were tacky and stiff from the dried blood that was caked on them – Big Mo's blood. He tried to ignore this and pulled himself over the side of the ferry and onto the deck.

The gas truck sat in the middle of the deck. Hopefully, Dubois had gassed up this ferry as well. Ray skipped steps as he scrambled up the slippery metal stairs. He had climbed steps like these more times, than he could remember, but never with such speed.

Dubois left the key in the ignition. Ray twisted the key. His heart slammed against his sternum, demanding to be free of the horror that had become Ray's life. The gas gauge moved to three quarters full. That would be more than enough.

Black smoke billowed from the smoke stacks as Ray slammed the throttle lever forward. These boats were never made to move fast, but with a massive diesel engine and nearly empty deck, Ray would be able to catch up.

Waves smashed into the bow of the ferry and foam spilled across the deck. Ray didn't care to try and navigate the waves with caution. All he cared about was catching up to Dubois and that damned sea monster.

The front of the ferry disappeared under another wave. Water splashed across the windows of the control tower, distorting the image in front of Ray. As Ray rode up the face of the next wave, he saw a huge, curved claw emerge from the water. The talons that tipped each digit dug into the metal deck of the ferry and dragged the boat into the trough between two waves.

If the sea monster kept Dubois and the kids down in the trough, the next wave was going to swamp the ferry and kill the engine. Then the only choice they'd have is to be eaten or to drown. Ray had to get the dragon to let go of the ferry so Dubois could guide it safely through the waves.

The monster's scaly head and serpentine neck rose above the waves. Two foamy jets of water sprayed from its nostrils as it pulled the ferry further into the wave. It clamped a second claw onto the stern of the boat.

On the crest of the next wave, Ray gunned the engine of his ferry. Black smoke swirled around the control tower. The ferry picked up speed. Gauges red lined and an alarm sounded from somewhere on the control panel. It was all background noise, just a distant clamor that Ray hardly noticed. All he could see was the monster.

The bow of Ray's ferry crashed into the back of the dragon. Its head reared back. A massive yellow eye glared at Ray through the windows of the control tower.

"Certainly got your attention now." Ray grabbed the polished wooden handle that sounded the ferry's air horn and pulled. A deafening blast filled the air. "Come and get it," Ray said. "This is where the good eatin' is."

The dragon turned its attention to Ray's ferry. The ferry carrying Dubois and the children disappeared behind a wall of dark water.

The front half of the monster slithered onto the deck of the ferry. Its weight began forcing the ferry beneath the waves. Ray threw open the door to the control tower and ran down the steps. The ferry jilted to the side and Ray stumbled. He caught the railing and pulled himself up.

The monster lunged forward, snapping its teeth with such force that Ray felt air rush past his back. He didn't need to look behind him to know that it was there. He had the creature's attention. Now he needed to finish this.

Ray opened the door to the gas truck and leapt inside. He shifted the gears into neutral, grabbed the doorframe and swung himself onto the running boards. A small ladder led to the top of the steel gas tank that sat in the bed of the truck. Ray climbed to the top of the tank. A circular hatch was set in the top of the tank. Ray grabbed the handle in the center of the hatch and wrenched it to the left. The unmistakable reek of gas assaulted Ray's eyes and nose. Fuel sloshed in the bottom the tank.

The creature climbed further onto the deck of the ferry causing it to tilt towards it. The fuel truck trembled and then rolled forward. Ray grabbed the open edge of the fuel hatch to keep from slipping off of the tank.

A tangled nest of crooked teeth gleamed in the sodium floodlights of the ferry. The fuel truck rolled forward. The screech of metal echoed above the wind as the dragon tore into the front end of the truck.

Ray stared into the monster's huge yellow eyes. A strange sense of tranquility settled over Ray. He was beyond being scared. He was pissed.

The hard plastic of the flare gun pressed into Ray's back. He grabbed it with his free hand and aimed it into the open fuel tank.

"This is for Big Mo and Cal." Ray pulled the trigger.

There was the loud *POP*. The *hiss* of the flare. Then there was nothing.

Dubois heard the children scream as the sea monster grabbed the stern of the ferry and pulled them back into the waves. The engine groaned and struggled to keep the ferry moving forward, but the monster was too strong.

A shudder passed through the ferry and then it was moving forward again. Dubois looked out the windows. The second ferry had rammed the dragon. Dubois thought he saw Ray at the controls laughing as the second ferry's air horn blared.

Ray was saving them, but Dubois knew that meant sacrificing himself. He wanted to stop Ray, to find some other means of ending this. There was none. Dubois needed to get the kids safely to the mainland. He waved to Ray. It was a simple gesture, but spoke volumes. Dubois gunned the engine.

An explosion lit up the stormy sky. Dubois rode up the face of the next wave and looked back to where the other ferry had once floated. Greasy smoke and flames danced across the water. A section of the ferry, little more than twisted metal, bobbed on the waves. The monster clung to the debris. Its neck lay limp across the wreckage, ending in a ragged stump. The dragon's lower jaw, bloodied and detached, skid across the deck and slipped into the waves. The rest of its body followed.

Dubois guided the ferry through the waves. Water smashed into the ship and slid across the deck, but Dubois no longer felt fear. The monster was gone.

Sickly amber light pierced the darkness surrounding the ferry dock. The storm waters had spilled over the seawall and into the streets. The dock was useless, either destroyed or submerged. Dubois spied an open section of shoreline that looked like it had been a beach. The ferry ground to a halt as Dubois beached it on the shore.

"Is it dead?" one of the twins asked.

"Is the dragon really dead?" the other added.

"Yeah," Dubois nodded. "I saw its body. Ray killed it. It's gone."

"Where's Ray?" Daniel looked towards the stormy ocean behind the ferry.

"He's gone too," Dubois answered. "Let's get the hell off this boat and go find some help."

"You know that no one is going to believe us," Cam said as he helped his twin sisters off the ferry. Daniel jumped down behind the girls.

Dubois knew Cam was right. No one would believe a story about a sea monster or a dragon. No one, except those who had survived it.

Epilogue

Days later, Sunset Island emerged from beneath the stormy ocean waves to be known as the greatest hurricane disasters in recent history. The sea had swallowed an entire town, as well as a cargo ship and oilrig. Little remained to tell the tale of what had been lost to the storm and the sea.

What remained of the sea monster and Ray had been swept out to the deep water, and had sunk to the bottom of the Atlantic Shelf, well beyond the prying eyes of man.

The broken hull of the *Ponce De Leon* rested on the edge of the shelf, rusting in peace and protecting a clutch of eggs from a creature no one believed to exist.

The End

CPSIA information can be obtained
at www.ICGtesting.com
Printed in the USA
LVOW04s1938151116

513060LV00010B/958/P